# A SCALED TRIBULATION

## BOOK ONE
### The Redemption Series

# Aaron D. Brinker

# ALSO by AARON D. BRINKER

The Narrative of Benjamin White
Second Chances
Mane of Redemption
Regaining Power

*Thank you to my beta readers:*
*Lisa Brinker and Tina-Marie Miller*

# PROLOGUE

Jerry Clarkson entered the parking garage as the daylight faded. Usually, the streets of Chicago were well lit around dusk, but the city had been experiencing rolling blackouts for the better part of a week. No one from the power company had been able to find the source of the problem. Jerry clicked on his flashlight as the last bit of light ebbed into darkness and began making his way towards the roof access.

As he ventured to the staircase, he caught the faint scent of cigarette smoke and sulfur. Jerry looked up to see the glowing embers of a cigarette end moving through the darkness. Lifting the flashlight, the beam revealed a man around his mid-40s. He was clean cut and well dressed. The only thing that looked out of place was a tattoo of a goat on the side of his neck. Jerry's voice quivered as he asked, "Who are you?"

The stranger took another drag of his cigarette. A wide grin slowly stretched ear to ear as smoke escaped his mouth. The man responded with a smooth baritone voice. "I believe, you'll have plenty of time to figure that out."

Knowing the type of business associates he kept, away from the office, he was not one to trust other freely. Jerry pulled a .357 Magnum Revolver from under his suit coat and lowered it to his side. "What do you want?"

The man raised the hand holding the cigarette to his face. He scratched his cheek with his thumb. He extended his arm towards Jerry, his index and middle fingers pinching the smoking butt. "And now we've arrived at the real reason I am here." He took a few steps closer to Jerry. He stood tall portraying total confidence. "You're going to wire all of the money that you've been laundering for the last 20 years to numerous accounts of my choosing."

Jerry laughed and raised the gun towards the man. The man lifted an eyebrow and sneered. Jerry fired a few rounds into the stranger. The man paused and, with a furrowed brow, looked down at his shirt. He reached into one of the oozing holes and pulled out a mushroomed bullet. The stranger held his hand in front of his face inspecting the fragment. "It's strange that even the heat of a freshly expended bullet still feels like ice." Crimson drops dripped from his fingers, splattering onto the floor. The man looked from his hand to Jerry, a frown marring his serious face. "This was my favorite suit."

Everything in Jerry, froze. It felt as if his heart had stopped beating and he lost the ability to breathe. The stranger carelessly dropped the bullet fragment, then lowered his arm to his side. Jerry's mouth hung agape in shock. He felt the control of his body slipping, almost like something else was taking over. Through no control if his own, Jerry's hand raised and pressed the searing barrel to his temple. "Let's weigh your options, shall we?"

A bead of sweat rolled down Jerry's face and spattered

onto his collar. "You could wire the money from your phone and live a little longer," Jerry's eyes shifted towards his raised hand, then back to the man.

"Or, you could pull the trigger." He felt is index finger tighten on the trigger slightly at the stranger's words.

"Either way, I'll still have your money before midnight."

Jerry's voice quivered in fear as he struggled to move his finger against the force controlling him. "Alright, alright I'll transfer the money, just release me and let me lower the gun."

The man grinned. "Fair enough." Jerry felt control return to his hand, once again, and placed his gun back into its holster. The Stranger took another drag off of his cigarette. "Go ahead then." He pointed at Jerry. "Transfer it."

"What accounts do I need to transfer the money to?"

The man took a slow drag off his cigarette. "That information will fill itself in as it is needed."

After a few minutes of typing and working on his phone, Jerry lowered his hands. "There, you have your money. Now, who are you?"

The stranger grinned. The blood drained from Jerry's face as he watched the man's mouth start emitting smoke without taking a drag from the cigarette in his hand. "You'll have that answered soon enough." He said with a smirk. "Thank you for doing business with us. We greatly appreciate it." He turned towards the corner and walked a few steps before stopping and turning to the shadows. "Make it quick and quiet." He said before walking away with a confident stride and vanishing into thin air.

Jerry suddenly was aware of the strange clicks and raspy breathing coming from the dark void to which the stranger had just spoken.

Out of the shadows Jerry saw a faint glow appear, which

quickly formed into an umbrella like shape. As he watched, the glow grew more defined to the point, he could make out what appeared to him to be lava-colored veins. The creature's mouth took shape as an orange throaty glow framed with sharp, silhouetted teeth. It's magma-colored veins shook as a bony rattle petrified Jerry to his core. From the beast's open maw, a glob of molten goo unexpectedly flew out onto Jerry's face, covering his mouth and neck. He tried to scream, but nothing came from his melted flesh through the molten slime covering what was once his mouth. His death came within seconds as the skin and bones of his neck melted; separating his head and torso. The mass that was once Jerry's head fell to the ground and rolled towards the monster. The creature folded the bony flaps back along its neck and stopped the rolling mass of melted flesh with its foot. The beast lowered its head and sniffed the ball of gore underfoot. With an eerie, almost laughing like sound, the creature raised its head and kicked the half liquefied skull across the parking garage.

# Chapter 1

As the cab pulled up in front of the apartment building, Jess looked over and smiled down at her two children, Justin and Charlie, sitting beside her "Daddy and I want you two to behave yourselves while we're visiting your Grandpa Christophe. Okay?"

The boys looked up at her with sweet smiles in response and said in unison, "Okay mommy

She ruffled the hair on the twins' heads and gave a pert smile. "Thank you. Now, let's head in and see grandpa."

Everyone shuffled out of the cab, Jess and the twins stood on the sidewalk while Adam helped the driver remove their luggage from the trunk. Adam handed the driver money for the fair plus a large tip. "Thank you for your patience."

The driver's face lit up. "Thank you for your generosity!" He said before quickly walking back around the cab, got in, and drove away.

Adam picked up the bags and walked towards his family. Jess took one of the bags from him to lighten his load. The family walked through the double glass doors into the lobby of the apartment building.

The Lobby attendant, an older man with a kind face, watched as the family entered. "Miss Jessica! It's been quite some time since I had the pleasure to see you." His smile stretched ear to ear with his upper lip covered by a thick, white mustache.

Jess dropped the bags and ran up to embrace the man in a tight, familiar hug. "Marco! That it has—it's been what—ten years? It's great to see you again."

They released each other and Marco turned to Adam looking at him with a playful critical eye before approaching him. The two shook hands as Marco smiled warmly and said, "Adam, you're definitely looking well." He turned looking at the twins then back at Adam with a playful wink. "And, multiplying! Lucky for them, they look like their mother."

Adam laughed. "I couldn't agree more." He motioned to the boy on his left. "This is Justin." Then, he motioned to the twin on his right, "And this is Charlie."

"Two wonderful young men. How old are they?"

Adam responded, "They are six."

"If they turn out to be anything like their parents, then they should grow up to be great men."

Jess blushed. "Thank you. They are well behaved and bright for their age."

"Bless my soul, they're already well on their way by the sounds of it."

Jess smiled and placed her hand on Marco's shoulder. "It was good seeing you again, but I'm sure dad is anticipating our arrival."

Marco's face furrowed before he looked down. "Actually, he is not upstairs. He left a message to give you the key to his apartment. There are times he doesn't return from work for days."

Jess nodded with a disappointed frown. "I should have expected as much. He has always been devoted to his work."

Marco nodded knowingly. "I'll get you the key."

Charlie tugged on Adam's hand. Adam looked down and asked, "What is it, buddy?"

"Are we going to get to see Grandpa?" Charlie asked with a worried look.

"Soon enough, bud. He's still at work right now." He looked up at Jess and saw the hurt in her eyes. "Let's head upstairs, so you boys can get to bed. It's been a long day."

The boys rang out in unison, "Okay, Daddy."

As they turned and started towards the elevator Charlie asked, "What floor does Grandpa Christophe live on?"

With a disappointed, flat voice, Jess said, "Grandpa Christophe lives on the 70th floor."

Charlie looked to Justin, both wide eyed. Adam looked at Jess with a worried look. The furrow in her expression eased. "You boys will be sleeping in my old room."

Justin looked up at Jess with an open mouth. "You used to live with Grandpa?"

Adam and Jess laughed. "Yes. I wasn't always this old. I was once your age many years ago."

Charlie asked, "How many years ago was that, 50?"

Adam pulled Charlie towards him playfully, mock whispering loudly enough for both his sons to hear "Careful, Charlie. It's never a smart idea to joke with a woman about their age. Remember that, it will save you a lot of arguments in the

7

future. okay?" Adam finished with a soft chuckle.

"Okay, Daddy. I'm sorry, Mommy." Charlie said with a sweet innocent voice.

Jess leaned over and kissed Charlie on the forehead. "That's all right, sweetie." The elevator finally arrived on the 70th floor with a ding. The four stepped off the elevator and turned left. The walls were a sky blue, a hunter green carpet ran the length of the hall, and a huge bay window was at the opposite end. Jess took the lead, guiding the family down the short hallway to the door at the very end. Once arriving at the door, Jess put the key she had been given in the lock and opened the door. As they stepped through the doorway and into the spacious Penthouse, the boys stood with mouths agape shocked at what they saw.

"How big is this place?" Charlie asked with a shocked squeak.

"It takes up half of the floor." Justin exclaimed at nearly the same moment his brother spoke.

"Wow. Can we get a place this big someday?" Both boys asked in unison with hope and longing in their eyes.

Jess set the bag down on the floor laughing at their joy and awe. "I hope so, sweetie." She escorted the boys to her old room down the short hallway. "Here's where you'll be sleeping. The bathroom is right across the hall." Adam set the boys' bag down on the floor. "I want you to get changed into your jammies and I'll put your toothbrushes in the bathroom. Both of you need to brush your teeth before bed."

Justin and Charlie replied in near perfect harmony, "Yes, mommy."

# CHAPTER 2

After the boys were in bed and sleeping, Adam and Jess sat down in the living room drinking wine, looking out over the cityscape through the large bay window, and talking. Due to acquiring his ability two years earlier, Adam could handle alcohol better without addiction being an issue. He thought this was mainly due to a heightened metabolism. Granted, he kept it to one drink on a rare occasion when he chose to indulge. He was still haunted by too many memories of what drinking in excess had almost cost him.

Looking over, he saw Jess mid-sip with glistening, wet streaks running down her cheeks. Adam reached over placing his hand on her knee in comfort. "Are you okay?"

Jess lowered her glass, sniffled, and nodded fighting the sorrow clearly showing on her face "Yeah. I just thought that he would have changed by now."

Adam set his drink aside and leaned over putting his arm around her in a comforting gesture. "I'm sorry, sweetie. Is there anything I can do to help?"

Unknown to them, Christophe had arrived home and eased the key into the lock. He was moving as quietly as possible since he didn't want to wake anyone, making an effort to make as little noise as possible. His hand gently turned the key and inched the door open. With every stealthy inch the door moved, Jessica's voice grew louder. He stepped in and shut the door without as much as a whisper. Not wanting to interrupt the conversation he quickly moved into the living room and leaned against the wall to the hallway around the corner.

Jess reached up and placed her hand on Adams. "Only this and listening. I wish all those years growing up, that I could have felt important to him. When he could detach himself from his work long enough, he was a great father."

She took another sip of wine, bracing herself to continue airing her feelings to Adam. "Scenarios like tonight were all too common for us growing up. His work was always more important." She swirled the wine in her glass and watched the dark wave, temporarily numbing herself of the pain.

Christophe lowered his head listening quietly until Jess began speaking once again.

"Granted, I never wanted for anything growing up, save one thing; the love and adoration of my father." She sniffled, wiped another tear from her eye, and then took another sip from her glass.

Christophe's slight movement shifted him enough that his form stepped into the reflection on the window from the doorway. "All I ever wanted was to give you a safe and wonderful life. I'm sorry for my shortcomings. It was never in my intension for you to feel unwanted."

Jess got up startled at the unexpected intrusion and went to her father hugging him tightly. "I never felt unwanted; only less important." She pulled away from Christophe's shoulder. "The times you spent with me when you were able to detach from work, when I was the focus of your attention, were some of the best times of my life."

Christophe gently placed his palm on Jess's cheek. "Allow an old man to make amends. I'll take a four-day weekend to spend every moment with all of you. We can take the boys to the Field Museum and maybe a Blackhawks game."

Jess lit up with hope and anticipation at spending some time with her father. "That would be great, it will be fun to spend some time together the next few days."

Christophe motioned towards the couch. "Why wait?" He glanced at the wine glasses on the table. "Give me a moment, I'll join you."

Adam and Jess walked around and sat back down on the couch picking their glasses up and settling. He returned moments later with a glass and the bottle of wine. He poured a glass and motioned to the others to see if they wanted more. Jess held her glass up accepting the gestured offer. Christophe began filling and she nodded when the quantity was to her liking. Christophe motioned with the bottle towards Adam.

"No thanks, Christophe. I usually try to keep my limit to one."

Christophe nodded as he set the bottle on the table. "Guilty conscience?"

Looking at Jess, who's face had quickly dropped at her father's comment, and placing his hand on hers, he said, "No. I just realized that some things are more important than that extra drink."

Christophe looked down at Adam's hand over Jess's. "Fair enough. I must admit, it is comforting to know that my daughter married such a wonderful man."

Adam lowered his head and raised it again slightly grinning. "Thank you, Christophe."

Christophe returned the smile and asked, "So, what are you up to these days?"

Adam took another sip from his nearly empty wine glass. "I'm still with the same company."

Christophe swirled the wine in his glass watching Adam with a curious look. "What was it you did there again?"

"I manage the accounts of clients we haven't heard from in the past three months. My job is to reestablish contact with them to see if they are still satisfied with our services."

Christophe took another sip of wine with a smile. "So, you're pretty much damage control."

"Not really. I just touch base and check on our client's well-being. If I come across anyone who's disgruntled, I send them on to Customer Retention."

"Why haven't you put in for promotions?" Christophe asked with genuine curiosity. "With your background you have the potential to be a CEO."

"Being a CEO would pull me away from Jess and the kids too much." Adam said smiling gently as he looked over at his wife.

Christophe's brow furrowed and his eyes narrowed. A second later they straightened and he gave a single nod. "Fair enough. At least, you're the type of husband and father I had wished to be." He patted Jess's hand that was resting on her knee.

Christophe quickly finished what wine remained in his glass with one gulp. He stood up and said, "I suppose, I had better be heading that way. I have a meeting first thing in the morning." He leaned over and kissed Jess on her forehead.

Adam's face dropped. "I'm sorry if that came out wrong. I didn't mean that as an insult."

Christophe smiled and placed his hand on Adam's shoulder. "I know you didn't son. I'm not offended. You've just shown that you are the man I had always hoped to be." He looked to Jess. "I just fell short of my intentions. Goodnight you two and sleep well. I love you both."

"I love you too, Daddy." Jess answered softly, her tone disappointed but accepting of his abrupt departure.

"Love you too, Dad. Sleep well." Adam said quickly watching as Christophe nodded his response then walked to his room.

# CHAPTER 3

**M**ichael approached the hooded figure standing along the shore. All but the bottom of the man's cloak was white, the area just above the sand was stained crimson. Christ's head was held high gazing upon the New Jerusalem bordering the opposite shore.

Michael stopped beside him and dropped to one knee. "You wished to see me, Lord?"

"Rise Michael. We have been through too much to require kneeling outside of ceremony." He grinned at the angel kneeling at his feet. "A salute will be more than adequate."

Michael nodded as he stood and slammed his fist into the left side of his breastplate and pulling his wings closer together behind him. A second later his wings relaxed and he dropped his hand back to his side. "How can I be of service?"

"On the contrary, the question is 'How can I serve you?'"

Michael lowered one brow. "I'm sorry. Did I miss something?"

Christ laughed. "Not at all." He turned his head and looked at Michael. "Walk with me, there is much for us to discuss."

Michael nodded and followed as Christ turned and began walking along the shore. "There is trouble brewing that must be stopped. Jude and Adam must once again keep the forces of darkness at bay. They will be tested more than ever."

"Is the threat that great?"

Christ looked out across the crystal waters and his brow furrowed. "Yes. The darkness on the horizon will test them more than any previous entanglement." He turned his head towards Michael. "Even you will be tested this time."

"How will I be tested, Lord?"

"You will know when the time comes."

Michael raised his head and took in the site of the gates to the city. Though Michael had looked at the walls of the New Jerusalem countless times, it had always been an impressive sight. The walls stretched farther than the eye could see in height and width. It consisted of colossal gemstones larger than any man or man-made building. They entered through the giant pearl gate with their voices echoing through the long corridor.

"This upcoming skirmish will bring death." Christ's voice broke the stillness.

Michael walked, mouth agape. "Will it be Adam or Jude?"

"That remains to be seen. It could be one of them, or neither of them." Michael nodded in understanding and acceptance at the Lord's words.

"You will also have more help with this battle than you

had before. I am granting another with a gift, and will let you know of this person's ability in due time. Lucius' new beast has already killed and will do so again soon." They stepped out into the light from the tunnel. "You must get to Adam and Jude to let them know. Jude will need to travel to Chicago immediately."

"Chicago?" Michael said curiously.

Christ nodded. "Lucius has chosen a new location to try and spread his physical reach upon the Earth. You, and the Redeemed, must cut off the threat before it has time to manifest into a larger force."

Michael nodded acknowledging the challenge ahead of him. "It will be done, Lord." Michael paused before asking the question on his mind. "Why do you call them 'the Redeemed'?"

Before the Lord could answer Michael heard the high-pitched laughter of little voices. He looked ahead of them and saw tiny heads bobbing up, down, back, and forth behind a hedge row. The green blind stood about two and a half feet tall. The laughter continued as they drew closer. A few steps further and six tiny bodies emerged from around the leafy wall. They smiled and ran toward Michael and Jesus as their laughter grew louder. Christ paused, smiled, and laughed. He picked one of the children up and hugged them.

Setting the child back down, Christ told them, "Go play." The child nodded and ran to catch up to their friends.

After a moment, after the children had run out of sight, Christ looked to Michael answering the question that had been spoken before they were interrupted. "They have been redeemed of their sins and as long as they do good in my name and fight for heaven, they will continue to be redeemed."

Michael looked down towards Christ's feet, pursed his lips, and twitched his head to the side. "That sounds logical. It would make it easier to refer to them as a collective rather than two individuals."

Jesus began walking again. "You must first meet with Adam and warn him of the impending danger. He must not act without you or Jude's presence."

Michael followed, walking alongside him. "I understand, Lord. I will go speak with him this very moment."

Christ grabbed Michael's pauldron and stopped him before he had a chance to dissipate. "It can wait a little while. There is more we must discuss. There will be more training involved for the two. They have been granted access to our training room until they are ready."

"Is it that serious to require the need of the Angel's training areas?" Michael asked in shock and worry.

Christ released Michael's armor. "Very much so."

They continued walking through the streets of the New Jerusalem. The people within the city constantly bowed until they were past. Michael knew if Jesus was staying quiet, it was for good reason. He followed along knowing that Christ had a point to staying silent. They continued climbing towards the center of the city and the palace. It was massive with no wall surrounding it. The great building was surrounded by a luscious landscape of emerald grass and small ponds around which people could congregate and visit with one another. The walls shimmered gold through a climbing, emerald wall of ivy.

They entered the front gates and walked their way through the corridors. Unlike the castle corridors of those on Earth during the Middle Ages, the palace corridors were not lined with the poor peasants living within the castle walls.

Every entity in heaven was equal. There was no class distinction other than Rescued Soul, Angel, and The Great Host.

"I know, you're wondering why I'm not speaking." Christ spoke, finally addressing the quiet atmosphere.

Michael nodded, acknowledging Christ's knowledge of his thoughts and feelings. "Yes, Lord. I know you have a knack for pausing for desired effect, but sometimes it is a little unsettling."

Christ placed his arm around Michael's neck in companionship. "You are very perceptive, and always have been Michael. That's what makes you such a feared warrior, and why you were the one I've chosen to lead the Redeemed against Lucius and his minions."

"I understand that Lord and I thank you for the opportunity." They turned a corner and entered the building Christ had guided them to. "The armory?"

"Yes, Michael, the armory." He walked over to a new piece of armor. It was silver with gold embroidery around the edges of the breastplate and pauldrons. The helmet was open faced with intricate designs etched into it and bordered with gold. Something seemed different about the armor to Michael. After a second, he realized what had seemed off. There were two wings attached to the back of the armor. They were folded in, but from what Michael could see they were patterned much like the other pieces to the ensemble. The metal feathers were silver flared with gold at the tips and the main arms of the wings were solid gold.

"I have something for you to give to Adam that he will need in due time." Christ said as he walked past the winged armor to a long display holding armor that was long and looked like a giant snake. Its color was that of a translucent pearl.

Michael reached out and touched a section of armor. He was stunned to find that it was quite solid. "Why the clear appearance?"

"That is temporary. We have made this armor special. It will change in different lighting to create a camouflage for Adam, but it will also shift with him. It could take the form of a hoodie or jacket while he is in human form, and will extend to the shape before you when he transforms."

"I'm sure he will love it. Is there anything else I need to know before I head out?" Michael asked with a serious cadence.

"Nothing other than an opportunity to speak with Adam is near at hand. Take it while you can." Christ said in warning.

Michael snapped to attention and saluted. "Thank you, Lord."

"Thank you, dear friend." Michael nodded acknowledging Christ's dismissal and vanished.

# CHAPTER 4

C had Robinson, a mob boss who ruled over a good portion of the southern part of Chicago with an iron fist, sat with his henchmen around the table. Cards and chips were scattered between them. The man to his left dealt cards to Chad, other three players, and himself. The two men to the dealers left threw in their blinds.

As the hand continued, Chad spoke out to the table. "How's everyone progressing?"

Voices proceeded around the table as three different tones rang out with, "Good."

The fourth man didn't answer. Chad continued staring at his cards. "Something wrong, Rick?"

"I've had a hiccup, but it's nothing to worry over." His eyes flitted up to Chad and quickly dropped back to the cards in his hand.

Chad pulled a cigar from his pocket and clipped the end. He placed it in his mouth and started turning it over. "Nothing to worry about, huh?"

"Nothing to worry about at all." Chad lit his cigar. "I've just got one person that is a couple days late on paying what's owed."

Smoke clouded over the table. Chad looked at his hand, upped the bet, and waited. Jason, a tall, gangly man with black hair upped the bet by $100.00. The other four threw their cards in the center signaling their folds. As Jason raked the pot closer to him, Chad took the cigar from his mouth and blew on the burning end until it was glowing. As poker chips clicked and clattered across the table, Chad shot his hand up and grabbed Rick's chin. Leaning his face in closer to Rick's ear, he said, "You will get the money and have it for me by tomorrow. Use force, if necessary. Do you understand?"

Rick's entire body and voice shook. "Yes, Mr. Robinson."

Chad said, "Good. Don't forget." He lifted his cigar, turned Rick's face a few inches away from him, and placed the burning end of the cigar to his exposed neck behind his ear lobe. As Rick screamed, Chad held the cigar in place for five seconds.

Chad removed the cigar from his neck and threw it on the table. Jason grabbed it and put it in an ash tray before the felt caught fire. Chad stood up and gathered a handful of Rick's hair. He released his chin and slammed his head onto the table and didn't allow it to bounce with the recoil. Chad spoke loud enough that everyone at the table could hear him. "If that money isn't in my hand by tomorrow, I will string you up and bleed you out like a dead animal. Is that clear?"

"Y...Yes, Mr. Robinson, Sir!" The men quickly responded in fear.

Chad released the man's hair and lifted him out of the chair by his collar. He kicked him towards the door. "Good! Now, get out there and get it. The clock is ticking."

As Rick neared the door, it opened and a figure stepped through wearing jeans, a hoodie, and a baseball cap. He grabbed Rick's shirt and stopped him from walking through the door. "Where are you off too in such a hurry? Why don't you stay here for a minute or two?"

"I...I can't. I have to go collect from someone." Rick turned and looked at Chad; pale faced and wide eyed. The newcomer looked at him with a smirk.

"It's alright, Rick. Stick around and I'll show you, first hand, what happens when someone doesn't pay their debt."

Rick nodded, looked at the man, and turned back to face everyone around the table. He raised his hand to cover the burn behind his ear. The new arrival patted him on the shoulder as he started walking towards Chad and the others.

Rick walked to the side and a few steps behind the man to see how everything would play out. The stranger glanced around the room as they approached silently counting the people sitting in the room. There were seven in total. Two men stood guard with semi-automatic weapons on balconies overlooking the room and the four that were playing poker at the table in front of him and Rick standing behind him. The strange man looked back to Chad with calm eyes as they neared the table.

Chad lit another cigar and Rick recoiled at the sight. "It's about time you showed your ugly face around here."

The man grinned. "I figured that it was high time that I graced you all with my presence."

Lines appeared on Chad's forehead as he scowled. "Do you know how much you owe me with added interest?"

The man shifted onto his right foot. He looked at Jason and lifted his eyebrows. "I'd say, close to a million?"

"That's right, Jack. I have to admit, you were always good with numbers. So, the literal million-dollar question is, 'Do you have my money?'"

Jack's mouth twitched into a slight grin. "No."

He looked across the table at Jason and tilted his head towards Jack. "String him up by his ankles." As Jason made his way around the table, Chad looked at Jack with a level glare. "I hope you like pain, my friend, you're about to experience a ton of it."

Jack raised his arms up to his sides as Jason walked towards him with zip ties in hand. "Sounds like a lot of fun." Jason escorted him over to a hook and chain hanging from the ceiling. As his feet were being bound, they brought over a chair. "Oh good, now it's getting interesting." After his feet were tied up, they sat him down on the chair and began hoisting him into the air by his ankles using the hook and chain. They lifted him until his head hung at about Chad's chest level. As Chad removed his suit coat, the man said, "You know, I've always loved when everything is inverted. The point of view is always so fascinating."

Chad back handed the man across the face causing his lip to split and leave blood dripping down his face. As Jack's body started to spin, Chad grabbed his shirt and stopped him. He pointed a finger in Jack's face. "If you want to stay alive a few minutes longer, you had best shut your mouth."

The man grinned playfully. "Oh, heaven forbid. I guess I'd better keep quiet, so I don't ruin your fun." He looked up on the balcony. "You boys comfortable up there? Be sure not to lock your knees." He looked back at Chad. "We don't need them to faint and fall over the edge. Now, do we, Chad?"

Another blow from the back of Chad's hand connected with Jack's face. "Oh yeah, I was supposed to shut up; wasn't I? My memory isn't what it used to be. Funny how that happens with age."

"You know, Jack, I used to like you, but you've grown to be an annoyance."

While everyone was focused on Jack and Chad's banter, Jack's reptilian tail snaked up the chain creating a double helix of iron and scales. When it was entwined enough to bear his weight, he placed the tip of his tail against the zip strips securing his ankles. The zip strips separated within seconds from the acid coated tail. He then held his tail out with the end pointing at Chad's head. He looked into Chad's eyes. "Hey, Chad."

Chad raised his eye brows. "What?"

"You're an annoyance as well." Jack allowed a few drops of acid to drip from his tail onto Chad's head. He wrapped his tail back around the chain to await the perfect moment.

Chad's eyes shifted from menacing determination to confused panic. As the acid ate deeper into his scalp, he began groping at his head trying to remove the burning substance. He stepped back and screamed as the pain only spread and got worse with his actions. As all of Chad's men, including Rick, swarmed in on him to figure out what was happening, Jack's tail unwound, and he dropped down from the chain.

As the two men on the balcony raised their weapons to begin firing, Jack flicked his tail in the air sending a glob of acid flying towards the balcony henchman closest to him. The projectile hit him in the chest with a wet plop and a sharp hiss as the acid began eating away at his clothing. Not realizing what was happening with Chad, he placed his hand directly onto the mucousy blob. He pulled his hand away from it and watched as the goo began to smoke and turn red as it ate away at his flesh. He screamed in shock, then dropped his gun and began tearing off his clothes trying to remove the burning substance.

Shots began ricocheting off of the concrete floor at Jack's feet in reaction to the attack and panic filling the room. Jack turned and sized up his overhead attacker. He picked up speed as he headed towards the staircase, never removing his eyes from the gunman. The man on the balcony hesitated in fear at Jack's next movement. As he approached the stairs, he made an exaggerated step on his left foot and leapt halfway up the staircase. He rebounded off of the handrail with his right foot and, in midair, whipped his tail around separating the gunman's head from his body.

As he landed back on the ground floor with both feet, he speared the base of the falling head with his tail. All of Chad's goons were still gathered around his body trying to figure out what had happened. A deafening roar shut their mouths all together. Their ashen faces turned to see a monster, standing below the balcony, with glowing frills extended from its head, and a familiar face piked onto the end of its tail.

They started reaching for their guns as the beast lowered its head and gave an almost human-like grin with a corner of its mouth. The creature began a slow hissing inhale. The longer it breathed in, the brighter the glow in its throat and frills grew. In growing horror and fear, the men began to fire their weapons only to be struck with terror as the bullets hit the beast's scales and dropped to the floor.

The men kept firing hoping to hit a weak point to take down the beast. They paused as the monster stopped inhaling and seemed to wink at them. Jason looked at the beast and said to the others, "We should have run when we had the chance."

The frills rattled and the beast unleashed a stream of molten material, blanketing the four men. The men began screaming and trying to scramble for something to save themselves as their clothes and hair ignited into flame.

Jack, still in beast form, began laughing a wicked, gravelly laugh as the men started dropping dead within seconds.

# CHAPTER 5

J ess left the penthouse at 11:30 am on her way to surprise Christophe for lunch. Her thoughts began wandering as she stepped onto the elevator. A huge part of her was hoping her father had truly changed, and this wasn't just an act to keep himself in her good graces. There were so many empty promises made through the years that, at a certain point, she began to give up hope.

She pushed the button for the lobby and the doors slid shut. "You know better than this, Jessica. What would make him care about his family, more now than before? It is probably just an empty promise to keep me quiet and distracted for now." As the bell dinged, the doors slid open to reveal the lobby and Marco looking her way from behind his desk.

His smile grew from ear to ear. "Miss Jessica! How does this day find you?"

She smiled in return as she approached his desk. "Hello Marco. It finds me very well."

"And where are you off to today?"

"I'm going to surprise my father at the office and treat him to lunch. Can you do me a favor if he calls, could you tell him that I am out?"

Marco placed his hand over the one Jess was resting on the desk and patted it. "I would be more than happy to. Is there anything else I can do for you before you head out?"

She smiled as she shook her head. "There is nothing that comes to mind. Thank you, Marco. I'll be back in a couple of hours."

"Sounds great, and enjoy the time with Mr. Christophe."

She stepped outside and hailed a cab. Ten minutes after telling the driver the destination, the cab pulled up in front of her father's office building. She paid the fair with an added five-dollar tip. "Thank you, Ma'am."

"You're most welcome. Have a great day."

"Yes Ma'am. You do the same."

She stepped out of the cab, and craned her neck to take in the height of Christophe's office building. It had been so long since she had been here, that she had forgotten its intimidating height. Her eyes lowered back to street level, and she entered the building's massive glass doors. Half of the space within the lower floor was open. The grey front desk stretched in a semicircle and was 25 feet in expanse, and allowed for four receptionists to sit comfortably. Behind the front desk were the multitude of elevators. Jess walked up to the closest receptionist.

"How can I help you today, Ma'am?" The receptionist she approached asked kindly.

"I'm here to surprise my father for lunch. I was wondering

if he was still on the same floor." Jess answered cheerfully.

The lady smiled, "Let me look and see if he is available for you. What is your father's name?"

"Christophe Picard."

The lady paused with a slight frown replacing the patient smile. "Mr. Picard doesn't like people showing up without an appointment. Let me call up to Shannon, his personal assistant, and see what she thinks." Jess nodded acknowledging her response.

The lady picked up the phone and punched in the extension. "Shannon? Hi, this is Casey at the front desk. I have a lady here that says she's here to surprise Mr. Picard." She nodded her head in response. "She claims to be his daughter." She lowered the receiver. "What's your name?"

"Jessica Campbell."

"Jessica Campbell." She nodded and smiled. "You're good to go. Shannon sounded as if she was jumping up and down. Head up to the middle elevator and go to the top floor."

Jess smiled. "Thank you, Casey."

"You're welcome, Ms. Campbell."

Jessica nodded and started towards the indicated elevators. As she arrived by the them, she pressed the button and waited. When one of the cars arrived, she stepped into it and pressed the button. A few seconds later the bell sounded and the door slid open to reveal a wide-open corridor leading to numerous offices with a receptionist desk in front of each.

She noticed a woman rise from her desk and start her way wearing a huge smile. Shannon ran up and embraced her like a relative would after spending years apart. She released her embrace and held her at arm's length. She spoke in a soft voice that Jess remembered so well. "It is so good to see you. You have grown into a beautiful woman."

Jessica blushed. "Thank you, and you haven't aged a day."

"How are you dear?" Shannon asked in a soft tone.

"I'm doing really well. I'm still married to Adam and have twin boys." Jess responded excitedly, glad to take a moment to catch up with her older friend.

Shannon's smile stretched even wider. "You do have pictures, don't you?"

Jess let out a short laugh, then pulled her phone from her pocket. "Of course, I do." She pulled up the pictures on her phone to show Shannon. "Here's what Adam looks like now."

Shannon's voice grew seductive. "Sweet Lord, Princess. He's still a hot one."

Jessica grinned with confidence. "That he is." She scrolled to the next photo and showed it to Shannon. "These are my boys; Charles is on the left and Justin is on the right. Twin boys… double the trouble."

"Oh my gosh, they are adorable. How old are they?"

"They are six and very intelligent. They're reading at a 9-year-old level."

"That is amazing. They say that children get their smarts from their mother." Shannon joked, nudging Jess playfully as she looked over the photos.

Jess blushed before putting her phone away with a smile

"Judging by them calling up, your father doesn't know you're coming, or just didn't mention it to the front desk?" Shannon asked as they moved towards her desk.

Jess shook her head. "No, he doesn't."

Shannon smiled. "Then, we're just going to have to remedy that, now, aren't we?" She walked around her desk and picked up the phone, then pushed a button, and waited. "Mr.

Picard? A lunch appointment just came in for you." She nodded as she listened. "I know you usually eat lunch in your office in order to get more work done, but you may want to
make an exception."

Jess could hear Christophe's voice through his door and
the receiver. "Who is that important to keep me from my
work?"

Shannon's brow furrowed as she saw Jessica's face drop.
Jess whispered disappointedly, "I see nothing has changed.
He always was more devoted to work than his family. It was
good seeing you again Shannon." Jessica turned with a scowl
and began walking away.

Her exit was interrupted when Christophe threw open his
office door. "Shannon, no one can be that important to keep
me from my work!" His face went blank when he saw Jess
turning around and looking at him. "Jessica."

"Apparently, nothing has changed. You are still too dedicated to your work to take a break to spend time with your
daughter. Enjoy your lunch. I'll see you when you get home."

Jessica turned to leave, and Christophe ran over to her.
"Honey, wait. If I had known it was you, I would not have
reacted the way I did." He placed his hand on her shoulders,
and pulled her in for a hug. "I'm sorry, Sweetie." He released
the embrace and held her at arm's length. Her face was fixed
in a scowl. "Shannon, cancel my appointments for the remainder of the day. I'm going to be spending it with family."

"Yes, Mr. Picard." Shannon replied quickly, turning with
a quick smile at Jess before returning to her desk.

Jessica turned to look at Shannon. "Thank you, Shannon."

Her face pursed into a smile. "You're welcome sweetie."

Jess walked over to Shannon and embraced her. "I want
you to join us for dinner tonight. It has been far too long, and

I want to catch up with you as well as with dad."

They released the embrace, but Shannon kept her hand resting gently on Jess's forearm. "I would love to. Just let me know when and where."

"Can do. It was good to see you again."

"You as well."

Jessica rejoined Christophe, and they headed for the elevators. They stood facing their mirrored reflections both not wanting to look at the other; Jess from disappointment and Christophe from embarrassment. After a few moments, Christophe looked at Jessica's reflection. "You were going to leave, weren't you?"

Christophe shivered at Jess's icy stare. "Yes, I was. I tried to surprise you by taking you to lunch, and my welcome was, exactly, what I've come to expect from you. Cold and unfeeling."

"I meant what I said earlier about my actions." He turned to her and she to him. He lifted her hands in his. "You mean more to me than life itself. I only hope that one day I can prove it to you."

She hugged him. "I hope so. The biggest thing is just showing me that I'm cared for more than your career." She pulled away and looked into his eyes. "Growing up, I always felt as if I was competing with the office for your attention."

He nodded and kept his gaze on the floor. "I'm sorry. There are a lot of things that I wish I had done differently while you were growing up. I missed out on so much, and it wasn't fair to you." The doors opened and they stepped off of the elevator. "I meant what I said last night though. I intend to start doing better by you."

As they stepped out onto the street, a tall, dark-haired man walked up to Christophe. "Christophe, I was just coming to see you." His voice was smooth and deep. His eyes shifted to Jess and then back to Christophe. "And who might this charming young lady be?" The man said with sly curiosity in his tone.

Jess looked at Christophe and saw pure terror in his eyes. "Roman!" Christophe stuttered. "I didn't know you had an appointment." He moved to partially step in front of Jess. "This is my daughter, Jessica."

Roman side-stepped Christophe and reached out his hand towards Jess. "It's lovely to make your acquaintance." When Jess reached around Christophe, she had intended to draw her hand back, but a radiating energy from Roman drew her away from her father. "You must get your looks from your mother." He glanced at Christophe with a critical eye. "Your father doesn't seem that handsome."

She blushed at the complement. "Thank you." For some reason, she found him quite charming and handsome. *There is something familiar about his scent. Why can't I place it?*

Roman released her hand. "I'll call and reschedule for… let's say… tomorrow?"

Christophe nodded. "Yes, tomorrow sounds good. I'll see you then." Christophe placed his hand on the small of Jessica's back and escorted her towards the restaurant.

Roman called at them as they walked away. "I'm looking forward to it. It was a pleasure meeting you, Jessica."

Jess asked Christophe as they hurried off, "Who is he?"

His answer came in a hushed tone, "Just a business associate."

"You're not in some kind of trouble, are you? I've never seen you so frazzled."

His aura calmed and his pace slowed. "No, sweetie. Everything is fine. I just have a project I'm working on for him, and haven't been able to meet the deadline.

# CHAPTER 6

Adam lounged on the couch in Christophe's penthouse with the boys sitting on the floor watching their favorite movie. He was hoping that Jess was having a good lunch with her father and building a better relationship with him. In all of the years they had been married, Jess had repeatedly confided in him about all the mental anguish her father had caused her while she was growing up. The knowledge that his work was more important than his family and numerous memories of Thanksgivings and Christmases that he had chosen to spend at the office instead of at home.

The boys laughed at a scene in the movie and turned to look at him. Adam smiled and laughed along with them while tapping the remote on his leg. As the boys returned their attention to the TV, a knock at the door echoed through the apartment. With the twin's attention drawn back to the movie, he got up and walked to the door to see who was there. Adam opened it to find Marco on the other side.

"Marco, hi." Adam leaned out of the door and looked down the hall. "Is everything alright?"

"Everything is perfectly fine, Mr. Campbell." Adam looked him in the eye. "I was wondering if you would meet me on the roof in about five minutes. There is something I need to discuss with you."

Adam glanced towards the living room and turned back to face Marco. "I have the twins with me and Jess is having lunch with her father."

"I promise you; they are asleep and will be so until you return from our discussion."

Adam raised his brow. "How could you know something like that?"

"I have my ways. If they are not sleeping by the time you are back in the living room after closing this door, I will speak with you some other time." Adam nodded and closed the door. As he walked back towards the living room, he was curious as to the validity of Marco's claim. To Adam's surprise both boys were sound asleep in front of the TV. He walked to the bedroom to get his socks and shoes.

There was something physically different about Marco that he could not exactly place at that moment, something familiar. He checked the boys one last time before locking the door and heading towards the roof. Adam took the elevator to the top floor and then the stairs to the roof access. Upon opening the door, he saw Marko standing at the edge looking out over the city. Adam slowly walked over to Marco and stood at his side. "I hope you didn't bring me up here to keep you from committing suicide."

Marco smiled. "No, Adam, I came here to keep *you* from

committing suicide." His face began to morph as Adam watched. As Marco turned to face him, Michael's familiar features became clear, it was those crisp, glacier blue eyes. Michael held out his arms. "Hello, old friend."

Adam stepped forward and embraced him. As they separated, Adam said, "What did you mean that you're here to keep me from committing suicide? For a second, after you revealed yourself, I thought it was your normal demeanor, but your expression says otherwise."

Michael's face lengthened. "A new threat has emerged. Lucius has found another pawn, and I have come with a message that you must not act alone. No matter what you see or hear, you must be patient. I will go speak with Jude and have him head this way, immediately."

"Why is the threat in Chicago and not New York?"

Michael shook his head. "I do not know, but just be vigilant. Christ isn't divulging all of the details to me yet, but he did say that this battle will bring pain." Adam's brow furrowed. "He's rather good at leaving out certain details, but I always know there is good reason behind it. As I said before, just be vigilant, and do not act until I have returned with Jude." Michael placed his hand on Adam's shoulder and smiled at him before disappearing.

Adam knew before he walked into the living room that he would find the boys still asleep in front of the TV. He sat on the couch watching them sleep while wondering what Christ meant by pain. Any encounter with Lucius entailed physical pain, either by him or his minions.

# CHAPTER 7

A few days had passed since Adam's rooftop conversation with Michael. He hadn't had much time to go out since the talk, but had been hearing minor stories on the morning news that sounded suspicious. Today, he planned to take the day to spend with the boys, but also to do some observing around the city. Jess had just left to go meet her dad for lunch again, and Adam got the twins bathed and ready to go for the day. He figured it would be a perfect time to spend some quality time with them. The more time they spent in Chicago, the more he realized he didn't spend near enough time with the boys. Adam had no idea where he would take them or what else they would do, but the city was big and full of fun things to do. He was sure it wouldn't take much effort to find a way to entertain the boys.

Justin was already dressed and waiting on the couch

ready to go. Charlie usually took a little longer to get around most days. He never wanted to be dressed identical to his brother, so he typically waited to see what Justin chose to wear for the day before he picked his outfit. Charlie had never liked it when Adam and Jess had dressed them the same, when they were younger. In some ways they always had wanted to be distinct from each other, but on certain issues they were undeniably alike. Adam's head appeared to hover in midair from the doorframe. "You almost ready to go, Charlie?"

Charlie grabbed another shirt from his suitcase, unfolded it, and put it on. As soon as the shirt cleared his head and he pulled it down he looked at his dad. "I am now." Charlie walked past Adam and out into the living room to join Justin on the couch. Adam shook his head while grinning and walked after his son.

He walked into the living room and over towards the front door calling out behind him as he reached for his coat. "Come get your coats on boys." As the boys came over and put on their coats, Adam donned his. He looked at the boys and asked, "What sounds better to the two of you, — pizza or hot dogs?"

The boys stopped fidgeting with their coats and looked at each other. They turned to Adam in unison. "Pizza!"

Adam gave the boys a big smile as he opened the door. "Sounds good. Let's get going." The boys walked through the door and he followed, closing and locking it behind him. They made their way to the elevator and down to the lobby. As they made their exit from the elevator, Adam looked at Marco. "Good morning, Marco. How are you today?"

Marco returned a wide smile. "I'm doing just fine, Mr. Crenshaw! What are you up to on this fine day?"

"I figured that I would take the boys out for lunch and have a look around the city while we were out."

Marco nodded. "That sounds like a wonderful idea. Be sure to be careful and bundle up. You don't want to catch your death out there." Marco's smile leveled slightly as he and Adam held eye contact.

Adam nodded. "We have our coats and will be sure to stay mindful of any nips in the air."

Marco smiled wide again. "That sounds great, Mr. Crenshaw." He looked to the boys. "You two be sure to look after your father now."

The twins smiled at Marco. "We will, sir."

Charlie asked, "Are you wanting us to bring you anything back?"

"What a little gent you are, Charlie." He placed his hand on the desk and leaned forward. "Thank you, but I should be all right for today. I have brought a sandwich from home for my lunch."

"You're welcome, Mr. Marco." Charlie leaned in towards Marco and pointed back towards Adam. "I'll try and keep him out of trouble."

Marco let go with a boisterous laugh. "I believe you will, Charlie. Just be sure that you two take good care of your father." Marco looked up to Adam. "He's a very special man."

Adam nodded and then heard Marco's voice within his head. "*Stay vigilant Adam. Lucius's minions are stirring in the most unlikely places. I will be speaking with Jude tonight. I will speak with you, at the latest, tomorrow morning on how soon he should arrive.*" Adam nodded again and ushered the boys through the front doors.

Adam walked out of the lobby with a tiny hand in each of his. He took a right and started heading towards the restaurant.

"What do you boys want on your pizza?"

Both boys said in unison, "Pepperoni."

Charles then asked, "Can we get thin crust?"

Adam laughed, "In Chicago? Only if you want to get thrown out of the restaurant. Chicago is the home of the deep-dish pizza."

"What do you mean by home?" Justin asked inquisitively.

"Chicago is where deep-dish pizza was created." Adam responded, proud of his boys for always working to expand their minds and knowledge.

"That's awesome!" Both boys answered in sync and excited to try something new.

"Yes, it is. I was thinking that maybe we can go to a hockey game while we're in town if you boys are wanting to go." Adam said watching and waiting for the boys' reaction to see if the idea might interest them.

The twins' faces lit up before Charlie chimed, "Can we really go?"

"Yes, we can." Adam's smile grew, glad that the idea of attending a hockey game excited the twins.

"Which team?" Justin asked, with interest.

"The Blackhawks. We'll have to see if they are playing a home game."

Charlie looked up at Adam. "That sounds good."

Justin jumped up and down. "Is hockey a slow sport?"

Adam laughed and looked to Charlie. "Nope. It's a fast-paced sport. Does that sound good to you?"

"Yeah, Dad. That sounds good." He paused for a second as they stepped past an alleyway. Charlie looked and saw a homeless man sitting on the ground a few yards into the alley. He started looking around and noticing more people in tattered clothes sitting down other alleys and against buildings.

He looked at Adam with a slight frown. "Are these people okay, Dad?"

Adam looked around and began noticing things that he hadn't before. One man lay face down sleeping, while on his back sat a large gangly looking demon with a body similar to Silverback Gorilla. Another man sat against a building with a change cup sitting at his feet for donations. A demon, similar to the other one sitting on the sleeping man, sat behind the second with the long arms wrapped around the man with the demon's arms crossed across the man's chest. A third man sat with his head down and twitching to the left. A demon similar in size to a small monkey stood on the man's shoulders, right hand on the man's head, and the left was jerking at the corner of his mouth. Adam realized the boys could not see the demons and answered Charlie with a gentle, caring tone. "They have just fallen on hard times. It's most often not the persons fault that times get tough. Sometimes very bad things happen in people's lives."

Justin looked up. "Did they deserve it?"

"No, Justin. In most cases, the people did not deserve it."

"Is there anything we can do to help?"

"Of course, there is. You can donate clothes, food to food pantries, and volunteer your time."

Charlie looked up at Adam. "Can we start volunteering when we get home?"

Adam rested his hand on Charlie's head. "We can look into it when we get home. You both are kind of young, but I am sure there is something we can do, together." He put his arm back at his side and Charlie slid his hand back in Adam's. "I'm very proud of you two. You are growing up to be very kind men."

As they stepped up to the next alley, Adam at first though

a wall was closer to the street than normal. With a second look he noticed it was not a wall he was seeing, but a mass of rotting flesh and bone. The demon was every bit of nine feet tall and five feet wide.

Adam had no time to react before seeing a form appear in midair with a flash of feathers, leather, and metal. The figure spun 180 degrees in midair and sliced the demon through from its left shoulder to the right side of its torso. The figure stood up, clasped his wings around his body, and turned to face Adam. A smirk crept across Adam's face. He whispered, "Michael, I should have known." He nodded to Michael and continued walking with the boys. Michael returned the nod as the Demon's severed top slid down its adjacent half and hit the ground spattering the alley walls with its charcoal-colored blood. Michael sheathed his sword as he turned to face the carnage.

Adam continued towards the restaurant; glad the twins were unable to see their hidden surroundings.

# CHAPTER 8

J ude stood in his usual stance, watching and listening to the city below. His rooftop viewing sessions had become a time of quiet reflection. He would calm himself between tasks of helping the lost. As soles lightly touched the rooftop, Jude's ears turned and his tail flicked. A wide grin stretched across his mouth. "Been busy the last few days, Michael?"

Michael stepped up next to Jude and placed his hand on Jude's tawny shoulder. "I never can fool you, can I? Did I even make a sound?"

"No, but it was your scent that gave it away. Your scent is one with no pollutants. It's pure." Michael nodded as Jude turned his head to face him. His face grinned wide and his teeth protruded as he breathed deep. "You're not here for a regular chat, are you?"

Michael shook his head. "No. There has been some trouble brewing in Chicago." Jude nodded. "We need you to head that way at your earliest convenience. Adam will need your help."

Jude lowered his leg from the roof edge and turned his entire body to face Michael. "Are he and the family safe?"

"Yes. I've told him not to act until you arrive, but to keep his eyes open for threats." Michael sighed and glanced away for a second. "I have been warned that this trial will test the team."

Jude's brow raised. "What trial isn't a test?"

"Christ just warned me that the team would be tested." Jude lowered his eyes to the rooftop. "Which means, that it is greater than your run of the mill skirmish.

Jude nodded and raised his gaze to meet Michael's. "Fair enough. Thanks for the warning. I'll speak with Simon and let him know to keep his eyes peeled." Michael nodded. "Let Adam know that I will be there as soon as I can pack and get on a flight."

"Sounds good. Your accommodations are already set. All you have to do is go to the ticket counter and they'll give you your ticket."

As Michael turned to leave, Jude said, "Thanks, Michael. Have you been made aware of what the threat is yet?"

"No, but I'm sure it is serious. I will be in touch once you reach Chicago." With that, he leapt into the air, spread his wings, and disappeared as an air current caught his wings and began carrying him off.

# CHAPTER 9

Jack ascended the few remaining stairs and opened the door to the roof. As the door swung open, he could see a woman, in her mid-thirties, standing at the edge of the rooftop overlooking the streets below. Her silky brown hair draped past the collar of the blazer that matched her short, blue skirt.

She had called him earlier in the day and told him to meet her at 10 pm. He raised his arm and glanced at his watch. As he nodded his head, he lowered his arm back to his side. After closing the door behind himself, he stepped up to her side and looked down at the cars and people below.

The woman gave him a sideways glance. "You're late." She all but hissed out at him.

"Only by fifteen minutes. What did you want?"

She looked out across the cityscape and followed the

lights of a helicopter flying over distant rooftops. "Rumor has it, that someone wiped out Chad's entire crew."

Jack nodded. "I heard that rumor as well." He looked up as her brow furrowed and she lowered her eyes to the busy street below. Jack looked through a window in the building across the street and saw a family sitting at the table playing a game. "You're not worried. Are you?"

"One organization gets taken out and you expect me to be worried?" she drawled out in an almost bored tone.

"You? No, I know you can handle your own." Jack said with a smirk.

She smirked. "I figured you'd say as much." Her smirk dropped. "The other, and main, reason that I called you was to inquire about the money you owe me." She looked over her shoulder at Jack. "This is your last warning. The next time my men will end you. Better yet, I may just take care of you myself."

He looked at her and nodded before she turned back to the city's activity. "I'll get it for you." He sidestepped closer to her.

"I know you will, Jack. I love you to pieces, but business is business." Her tone dropped from a playful lit to a dangerous growl.

"I understand. Business is why I needed the loan in the first place."

Raising a questioning well-manicured eyebrow, she gave Jack an inquisitive look. "What is it you want most in life, Jack?"

His gaze rested on the street below. "At this moment?"

"Yes, Jack, at this moment." She purred out, her curiosity being nearly palatable.

A beastly hand sank it's claws into her back on either side

of her spine. "To hear you scream."

Paralyzed with shock, her eyes were wide with terror and confusion as a tear rolled down her cheek. He pushed her over the edge allowing gravity to pull her to the pavement below. Her screams echoed through the surrounding streets, through windows and off building walls.

# CHAPTER 10

The next morning, Adam and Jess took the twins to the Chicago Field Museum. Christophe had a business meeting he could not cancel and said he would meet them for lunch afterwards, at a restaurant the boys would enjoy. The boys were eager to see all the artifacts and learn a lot of historical facts that they had not known. They paid for entry and began taking the boys around to see the exhibits. Justin and Charlie began running from each exhibit to the next, exhilarated by all the new information. Their eagerness never waned and continued to climb with each new sight. At the extinct bird exhibit, they stood in awe of how many species used to inhabit the Earth. Charlie looked at Adam, "Why did they all have to die?"

Adam looked at his son and noticed tears welling. He said, "I don't know, buddy. Humans are selfish and greedy.

They mostly look at expanding opportunity and making money. They don't realize what the advance of the Human Race is doing to other creatures that share the planet."

A tear rolled down Charlie's cheek as he blinked and looked back towards the display. "I wish people would learn from the past."

Adam rested his hand on Charlie's upper back. "Me too, son. Me too."

They continued further on and the boys were mesmerized by the exhibit that Adam wanted to visit most, the Lions of Tsavo. It wasn't much, other than the skulls and taxidermied skins of the lions that went on a rampage in the late 1800's attacking men in the Tsavo region of Western Africa. The twins stood in awe at the size of the skulls and teeth. After a few minutes, the family started to walk towards the next room of the Museum. As they stepped through the opening, Adam caught a familiar scent. He turned to see Lucius walking through the opposite entrance of the room. He stood in the archway facing Lucius, smelling the suffocating scent of sulfur that hung in the air. Lucius smirked and strolled over to the lion display. Adam shifted onto the balls of his feet, ready to attack, but another figure appeared in the adjacent entrance. He looked to see Michael, dressed in Earthly clothes walking in with a casual gate. Michael nodded acknowledging Adam and indicating he would take care of the issue. Adam returned the nod and then noticed Michael's hand at his side waving him to continue with Jess and the boys. Adam quickly left the room to catch up to his family keeping his ears and senses open in case something escalated.

Michael stepped up next to Lucius. They stood facing the lions. Lucius sighed with a smile. "Ah, you remember how much fun these two were?"

"Fun? You know how much work you caused me during that time. I lost count of how many trips I made while these two were on their killing spree."

Lucius inhaled with a hiss and laughed with a guttural growl. "I have to admit, I had a blast hearing the screams of their victims as they witnessed their own carnivorous demise. The numerous trips for you were an added bonus."

Michael turned towards Lucius. "What are you here for?"

"What am I always here for? To be a thorn in your side and further my reach. I felt like having a little fun today."

Michael's voice acquired a greater tone of authority. "What have you done, Lucius?"

His pupils reddened and his pointed grin stretched. "It's not what I've done, but what I'm about to do."

Michael caught movement out of the corner of his eye in the lion exhibit. The skulls were moving towards the pelts. Michael stood transfixed as the skulls turned and the mouths of the pelts widened. As if inhaling the skulls, the pelts swallowed the skulls whole. Michael gasped through gritted teeth as he realized the skins didn't swallow the skulls, but only set them in place as the heads began to twist and began forming muscle tissue. The heads were not all the changes taking place; the pelts were lengthening and growing back to the lions' original size. As the changes began to slow to their completion, the lions began looking around and stretching their mouths wide, baring teeth and smelling the air.

Michael spoke with Adam telepathically, *"Get Jess and the kids back to Christophe's now! Don't leave the apartment unless it's absolutely necessary. Jude should be on his way soon. No matter what you hear, do not leave that apartment."*

Adam started escorting the family at a quickened pace from three rooms away. "We need to head home now.

Something has come up, and we need to get back to Grandpa Christophe's." Shattering glass and a deafening roar could be heard from a few rooms over.

# CHAPTER 11

T he door to the diner opened and a man stepped through. He had a fair complexion except for three massive scars spanning diagonally across his face. The man stood to the side of the doorway to allow patrons the freedom to come and go as they pleased. His eyes searched the tables and booths for a familiar face. A hand to his left shot up as a baritone voice rang out, "Simon!" Simon looked towards the movement to see a well-built man sitting in the booth lowering his hand. He nodded and started walking towards where the man was seated.

As he sat down, Jude asked, "Did you forget what I looked like?" A smirk plastered on his face.

"In human form? Yes." Both men laughed.

"And if you remember correctly, I haven't seen you in human form since we first met."

Jude nodded while still grinning. "Good point." He looked up as the waiter arrived at the table.

The young kid assigned to wait on them looked to be about 19. Tall and lanky, he had dark, wiry hair that hung over his glasses. The name Sam was written on the nametag pinned to the front of his dirty uniform shirt. "What would you like to drink, Sir?"

Simon looked him in the eye with a polite smile, "Hello, Sam. I would like a coffee and glass of water, please."

"Sure thing. I'll be back with those in a minute."

As Sam walked away from the table, Simon looked at Jude. "So, what's the reason for this unexpected meeting? I'm pretty sure it's not just to catch up."

Jude took a sip from his coffee cup. "With how much I'd like for it to be a friendly get together, I'm afraid you're right." He looked up as Sam was returning with Simon's drink order.

"Here you are, Sir. One coffee and water. Do you know what you would like to eat?"

"Yes, thank you. I'll have a BLT with extra bacon on wheat please."

Sam began writing on his notepad. "Would you like chips or fries with that?"

"Fries, please."

"Very well. I will get this put right in for you." He finished writing and held out his hand to Simon.

"Thank you, Sam." He handed the menu to the waiter.

Sam took the menu and said, "You're welcome, Sir."

As Sam walked away from the table, Simon looked back to Jude determined to find out why he was summoned for the meeting. Jude enclosed his coffee cup between both hands. As he looked down into the steaming liquid he said, "My contact has informed me that a threat has manifested in Chicago." He raised the coffee cup to his mouth and took another drink. He lowered the cup back to the table and continued. "I'm taking the six o'clock flight. Adam is there and knows I'm on my way."

Simon poured sugar and cream into his cup. His brow furrowed. "Is it that serious of a threat?"

Jude nodded. "I need you to keep an eye out, in my absence, for anything more unusual than normal."

Simon nodded. "Yeah, sure thing. I can call you if I notice anything."

Jude shook his head. "That won't be necessary. If you really need to get a hold of me, feel free to, but anything non-life threatening, you can let me know about when I return."

Sam approached with Simon's food. As he set the plate down in front of Simon, he said, "Here you are, Sir. Does everything look alright?"

Simon looked up to Sam. "It looks great. Thank you, Sam."

"You're very welcome, Sir." Sam walked away leaving Simon to enjoy his lunch.

Simon motioned towards his food. "Are you wanting any?"

Jude shook his head. "No, thank you. I ate before you arrived."

Simon smirked. "That hungry?"

Jude shook his head. A dark complexion shadowed his face as he looked towards his coffee cup once again. "No. To be honest, I've been here most of the morning."

"That worried about Chicago?"

"To be honest? Yes." He looked up from his cup to Simon. "I'm not looking forward to another run in with Lucius."

"Lucius? What makes him so threatening?"

"Lucius is the worst enemy imaginable."

Simon smirked. "Do you mean figuratively?"

Jude locked eyes with Simon. "I mean, literally."

Simon grabbed a fry from his plate and pointed to Jude with it. "Do you mean to tell me that Lucius is the Devil?" Jude nodded as Simon consumed the fry. "How can we ever expect to defeat him? I know he can't, technically, be defeated. How can we at least keep him, physically, out of the Earthly realm?"

"With higher power."

Simon laughed. "Yeah, right."

"Do you think my gift comes from freaking leprechauns?"

Simon laughed as he shook his head. "Apparently not." As his laughter subsided, he said, "I know in our last run in you mentioned your connections are always watching. I had just figured that you were some sort of science experiment the Government had released to help control rising crime rates."

Jude laughed loud enough to cause heads to turn at nearby tables. "Is that what you've been thinking this entire time?" Simon nodded. "Forgive me. I'm not laughing at you, just at society and anything vastly out of the norm being blamed on a government conspiracy. My gift is divine," Simon's brow lowered on one side. "…celestial."

"Do you mean to tell me, that you have been gifted this ability from God?" Simon asked, the realization flashing across his face of what Jude being divinely granted these powers actually meant.

"Yes." Jude said with all seriousness.

"How did you manage that?" The clear awe apparent in his tone.

Sam arrived at the table and warmed their coffees. Jude grabbed a sugar packet from the caddy. As he ripped open an end and poured it into his cup he looked up at Simon and said, "Due to our first meeting."

"What do you mean?"

"Your big hand and those brass knuckles clocked me so hard it almost killed me. Because of my selfless actions that night, God saw fit to give me this gift to continue to protect the weak" His shoulders rose and fell with a sigh. "…and apparently all of humanity, considering Lucius's recent antics."

Jude looked at his watch and then reached for his wallet while motioning for Sam. "I have forgiven you for that night, so don't beat yourself up over it."

Sam stepped up beside the table. Jude handed him a hundred-dollar bill. "Here you go. This is for both of our meals."

"Yes, Sir. I'll be right back with your change."

"Keep it."

Sam's face went white and slack. "Sir?"

"Use it however you need to, be it to better yourself, or your situation."

Sam's face lifted a mile. "Thank you, Sir. You are a God send." As Jude gave a single nod, Sam turned and left to cash out the orders.

Jude raised his coffee cup to his lips and spoke loud enough to be heard by Simon. "You have no idea." Jude looked at Simon with an impish grin. Lowering his cup, he put his wallet back in his pocket. "Well, I'd better get home and get packed." As he rose from the table, his brow furrowed. "Remember to stay mindful, and do not confront anything you see other than crimes. What we're facing can literally appear from nowhere."

Simon nodded and shook Jude's hand. "Safe travels my friend."

# Chapter 12

Lucas Hester walked through the restaurant doors into the brisk, evening air. He angled right and walked along the street towards home. A man bolted from the restaurant and ran after him. "Luke!"

"What do you want, Omar?"

Omar waited a few seconds to see if he would turn to face him. Luke kept facing the way he was travelling. "You wanting me and a couple of the others to escort you?"

Lucas smirked and looked up. "Is that worry that I hear in your voice?" He asked in a sarcastic tone.

Omar shook his head. "Yes, Sir. There's been at least three people killed in the last few weeks."

Luke sighed in exasperation. "You act like that's new news to me."

Omar just stared at him. "Do you want us with you?"

"I'll be fine." He turned and started walking away. "If you're that worried, you can follow me in the car." He continued walking ahead and Omar went back inside to get a few of his comrades. As they walked to the car, he voiced his concern to the others.

They spotted Luke walking along the street on the sidewalk. He breathed a sigh of relief as Luke looked over his shoulder. They followed in silence for the remainder of his walk home.

As he climbed the stairs and inserted his key into the door, a ball of flame erupted through the door. It collided with his head with enough force that it catapulted him over the parked cars and into the middle of the street.

The henchmen stopped the car 20 yards away from him. They could see his chest rising and falling as he tried to breathe through charred lungs. Luke's face was upturned towards the sky. His entire body began shaking as he began to seize.

Omar and the others grabbed for the door handles. They had the doors part way open when they noticed a huge mass emerging through Luke's front door and pulled them closed as quietly as possible.

Omar yelled from the back seat. "What the heck is that?"

The driver turned and punched him in the face. "Shut up, Omar." He quieted and raised his hand to the area of his face, now throbbing. "Are you wanting to let it know that we're in here?" He turned back to the scene playing out before their eyes.

The monster looked in their direction and all four men sank further into their seats. It walked down the stairs and slowly turned its head back towards Lucas. It stepped up onto the hood and trunk of two parked cars and dropped down with little to no movement from the rest of its body.

Its frills crept open as it approached Lucas. They were extended when it leaned over his prone body. It looked up and into the car at the others and grinned. The driver of the car whispered, "Did that thing just…what is it doing?"

The beast looked back down at Luke and paused. Omar's pants became drenched, with what had been the contents of his bladder, as the creature sank its teeth into Luke's chest and tore a chunk of flesh, bone, and cartilage away from his body. It dropped it to the side and bit into Luke again, severing and pulling his heart away from his body. It rose up and looked into the vehicle, holding the heart between its teeth. The men were too scared to move. The driver began crying as an orange glow emanated from the beast's throat and Luke's heart began smoking.

The monster laughed as it tilted its head back and swallowed the burning heart. It breathed deep and the driver accidentally locked the door in his panicked attempt to exit the car and run. All four of the men paused as the creature stretched its arms and then waved at them with one of its hands.

Its frills began to glow. It slammed its body down, stretched its neck as far as it could, and rocketed a stream of lava through the windshield. The men screamed for a split second before the fuel in the tank exploded. The heat from the blast caused some of the fuel in cars parked close by to erupt as well. The cars lifted off the ground in a chaotic synchronization that had no specific rhythm.

The beast straightened up, gave a quiet laugh, and fled from the scene.

# CHAPTER 13

L ucius sat sipping coffee awaiting his pawn. The diner was slow with only a handful of people scattered through the dining area and bar. He wore a pointed grin as a young couple two booths over sat with the boyfriend degrading the young woman. The man sat in the seat facing him and made glances over the woman's shoulder as he berated her.

"You know that no one else would ever want you?" The woman looked down and recoiled. "You, see? You're unable to take criticism without cowering. You're hopeless, pathetic, and worthless. Lucky for you, I'm willing to look past all of those flaws." He caught a glimpse of Lucius smirking at him over the woman's shoulder. "What's so funny old man? Why don't you leave your ears out of this conversation and mind your own business?"

Lucius nodded while holding his coffee cup in both hands. "You have no idea how much of 'my business' it truly is. All evil in this world is my business." He returned his gaze back up to the man in the booth.

The man gave a nervous laugh. "Are you a freaking psycho?" The woman laughed. The man's smile dropped as his arm rose, backhanding her across the face. "Who told you that you could laugh?" The woman held her face in her hand and silently wept. The man threw a napkin at her. "Oh, dry it up, crybaby! You're so worthless."

Lucius began laughing loud enough to turn heads that were anxiously attempting to remain averted. The man flew out of the booth and towards Lucius. "I told you, old man, to mind your own business. Now, I'm going to give you worse than what I gave her."

The woman ran over to the man. "Mark, don't! He didn't mean anything by it." She was grabbing at his arm and looked at Lucius. The side of her face was already beginning to bruise. "Didn't you, Sir?"

Mark pulled his arm out of her reach and struck her to the floor with a closed fist. "You should know your place. I'm through with you. Good luck finding someone else who is willing to accept your insignificance!" The girl lay unconscious. Mark turned towards Lucius. "I warned you. Get ready for a beating."

Lucius took a sip of his coffee. "Listen, Mark, I'm going to give you one chance to walk away with your life. No questions asked." He gave him a sideways glance.

Mark laughed. "You're giving me a chance to walk away with my life? You must be out of your mind." His fist clenched in preparation for the coming onslaught.

Time stood still. All actions in the diner were frozen mid-movement. Mark couldn't move his hands and realized the only part of his body that he could move was his eyes. Lucius slowly rose from the booth and stood nose to nose with Mark. Lucius could see the fire burning in his eyes and inhaled deep. "My dear boy, you're not fooling anyone. You wreak of terror."

Tears began rolling down the man's cheeks. A forked tongue shot out of Lucius's mouth and caught one of the tears. As the tongue slowly retracted, the tear shimmered at the split like dew on a leaf. The tongue stopped and raised the tear to eye level. Lucius looked down at the tear and back into Mark's trembling eyes. The tips stretched, then curled in on themselves, and the roll continued until his tongue was behind jagged teeth.

When Mark looked back into Lucius's eyes, they were crimson. "The taste of fear is pure bliss." Lucius purred out grinning a serrated smile. "Now, my dearest boy, I will give you a chance to live or die."

Mark's eyes fluttered with a ray of hope. Lucius raised his hand, palm out.

"Don't get your hopes too high." He waved it to the side and placed it in his pants pocket. "There is nothing you can say or do to change the outcome."

Lucius sat back down in the booth. The other patrons began their nervous movements once again. To them, it looked like he was trying to decide whether or not to hit the stranger in the booth. Lucius spoke again so that everyone in the diner could hear him. "I'll say it one more time, I'll give you a chance to walk away with no questions asked." He didn't bother looking up. He just kept staring into the cup of coffee in his hands. "What's your decision?"

Mark's fist unclenched, then he turned and walked towards,

and out of, the door. What the diners couldn't see, was that he was being controlled by some outside force. No matter how much he wanted to struggle against it, he was powerless. With the progressive rise and fall of his feet, he moved towards the busy four-lane street. Tears streamed down his face as he continued through the first three lanes. *One more, I'm almost there. I just need my...*

The grill and front bumper of the Lincoln Navigator connected with enough force to throw Mark out of his shoes and 30 feet from where he had been. The driver had been texting and doing 20 miles per hour over the limit.

All the patrons and Lucius, for show, all stood and went to the windows. Lucius turned to wake the unconscious girl. "Elaine." He caressed her cheek with his thumb. "Elaine." Her eyes slowly opened. "Are you okay?"

She slowly nodded. "What happened? The last thing I remember was Mark trying to threaten you."

He helped her into a sitting position. "He punched you in the face and knocked you out."

She looked around frantically. Elaine looked back to Lucius. "Where did he go? He didn't hurt you, did he?"

Lucius shook his head. "No. Someone as small as him couldn't come close to harming me." He slid his arm under Elaine's legs and the other behind her back. He lifted her and placed her in the booth across from his seat. To Elaine, people outside of the diner were going on about their normal lives.

Cars and people passed by with no hint of the din actually unfolding in front of the restaurant. She could only see the people within the building going about their work and meals with a nervous unease. She thought it was due to the scene that had just happened with Mark. Lucius sat down across from her. "You are now free of him. What do you think you will do now that you no longer have to answer to him?"

Elaine looked down at the table for a few seconds. "I want to act. I've always dreamed about being on stage or in front of a camera. I just never had the money. While I was trying, Mark and I got involved and he pulled me away from it."

Lucius' lip rose. "Well, now you are free, and you have all the time you need to follow your dream."

She shook her head and looked up into Lucius's eyes. "I don't know where to begin. It's been well over a year since I've even auditioned."

"I've always found the place one left off is always the best jumping off point for a new beginning. Trust in yourself, hold tight to confidence, and keep pursuing." She nodded. "Now go ahead and get going and start living your dream. There is one condition, I may need to call on you in the future to help me if certain situations may warrant it."

"I would be happy to help you if you needed it. Thank you, Sir."

Lucius grinned a straight smile with normal teeth. "You're very welcome, Elaine." She maneuvered out of the booth and through the diner door never seeming to realize that the strange man knew her name even though she never introduced herself. Lucius took another sip of his coffee.

# Chapter 14

Fifteen minutes later, Lucius's pawn arrived. He walked up and slid into the booth across from Lucius. "What's all the fuss about?"

Lucius turned and glanced at the cluster of emergency vehicles. He laughed. "Just someone who wanted to pick a fight." He turned back to the man and raised his eyebrows before lifting the cup to his mouth grinning.

"Person must have been an idiot."

"I gave him a few chances to back down. The poor fool refused. Little did he know it was the start of the rest of his eternity." His index finger tapped against the lip of his coffee cup. "It took you long enough."

"Yeah. I got held up at the office for a few minutes longer than I expected." Lucius nodded.

The waitress approached the booth. "Do you need a

menu, Sir?"

The newcomer shook his head. "No thank you. I'll just have a cup of coffee, a cheeseburger, and fries."

The waitress began writing the order on her pad. "What would you like on it dear?"

"Lettuce, pickle, and mayo, please." She nodded and turned to go put the order in.   He looked to Lucius. "Why have you called me here?"

"I have another job for you, but this one is personal to prove your loyalty." The man nodded as the waitress returned to the table with his coffee. "This one will be difficult, but will prove that you will not falter." They both took sips from their cups. "The last person I had working for me ended up betraying me and is now helping our enemy. I am wanting to be sure that doesn't happen again."

The man's brow furrowed. "I don't plan on joining the other team. I've got too much to lose and so much to gain."

Lucius' gave a serrated grin. "That's good to hear, but we'll see your true resolve soon enough. I've given you powers beyond belief and shown you the path to make you a success."

The man nodded. "I'm grateful for all the gifts you've given me. What's the job?"

Lucius leaned in close across the table while holding his coffee cup in both hands. "I want you to kill your family." He turned and looked at the emergency response vehicles and back to his pawn. "And, you better not fail or betray me."

The man turned and looked at the scene unfolding across the street. His mind reeled as he contemplated the gravity of Lucius's words. He knew that he would not betray Lucius, but had not expected to have to kill part of what he was afraid to lose. The waitress walked back up to the booth and set the man's food in front of him. He looked at the plate, face blank. He looked up at the waitress and nodded. She walked away. Staring at the void where the waitress had just occupied, he asked. "What's in it for me?"

"What do you mean?"

He turned to Lucius with fury in his eyes. "What's in it for me? There were two reasons I made the deal with you. The first was to have more contact with my family and the other was abundant wealth and power. If I kill my family, I am destroying one of the reasons why we made the deal. So, once more, what's in it for me?"

# CHAPTER 15

As the plane came to a stop at the terminal, Jude waited patiently as the other passengers in the rows ahead of him slowly disembarked the plane, watching them leave until it cleared out to his row. He stood and removed his bag from the overhead bin, carefully watching that he didn't hit the older lady in the row behind his own. The entire flight, he had been overhearing the conversation a few rows in front of him. The husband had been verbally abusive to the wife. He had told her she was worthless and he could find better. The man promised her in whispered tones, that as soon as they reached the house, he was going to beat her until she was black and blue. Jude had spent the entire flight listening to this man go on and on, while he thought no one was able to hear him. At the same time, he smelled the woman's fear rise to the point she was starting to perspire.

Jude followed behind them while departing from the air-craft. He stayed about six to eight people behind the couple until they were in the terminal. He followed them to the baggage claim and waited. As the buzzer rang on the carousel the man said, "Go get the bags." The woman walked up to the carousel and waited.

Jude stepped up next to the man. "I have to admit, that was one of the rougher flights I've been on."

The man looked at him. "Does it look like I care?"

Jude leaned in. "No, it doesn't," He placed his hand on the back of man's neck and with a sudden transformation of his nails on his thumb and index finger pierced the man's neck below the base of the skull. The mark was left. "...but you will remember this conversation. Those piercings will explain themselves in due time." His eyes flashed his golden lion's eyes for a second, long enough for the man to notice, then returned to their normal green. The man stepped back rubbing his neck and checking his hand for blood. Jude smirked. "No worries they're already healed." The wife stepped up with both of their bags. "Have a nice day." Jude turned and started to walk away.

The wife turned and pointed towards the baggage carousel. "Aren't you going to get your bag?"

Jude lifted the bag in his hand. "I already have."

# CHAPTER 16

J ude ended up taking a cab from the airport. He decided to stop by a restaurant for a bite to eat before heading over to meet with Adam. What they were facing had to be pretty serious if Michael and the Almighty had him trekking to Chicago to help out. He felt confident that, whatever it was, they would be able to handle it.

As he walked up and down the streets looking for a place that sounded appetizing, he heard a faint cry from an alley. It sounded like a child's whimper and as he walked away from the closest dark recess, it grew more distant. He turned and headed back to the alley opening. His eyes focused and peered into the dark. "Is anyone there?"

A faint voice responded. "Yes. Could you help me? I'm so cold."

Jude could not make out where the voice was coming

from. His eyes altered to see more clearly. At the very back of the alley, against the wall, where it came to a dead end, a small silhouette could be seen. Staying alert and keeping his steps calculated, he proceeded with caution. As his progression lengthened, the silhouette grew more visible. He stopped when he was within 10 feet of the figure. "Are you okay, little one?"

A meek voice echoed off the walls, "I am now that you're here."

"What kind of help do you need? If you're hungry, I can get you something to eat. If you need clothes, I can get those as well."

"No, all of that is fine. I'm well taken care of." The child's voice then started a slow laugh that sounded similar to the subtle voice it had been speaking with over the last few minutes. Jude's hair stood on end as the laugh grew louder, deeper, and maniacal. Jude adjusted his stance to make sure he was as balanced as possible. The figure rose and shifted into a man. He slowly started walking towards Jude. "Jude, always ready to help a fellow man in need." A match sparked to life illuminating its owner's face as it lit a cigarette.

"Hello, Lucius. Long time, no see." Without removing his eyes from Lucius, Jude did a quick check with all of his senses. "How are the wife and kids?"

Lucius emitted a slow laugh. "Always love your sense of humor, Jude." He took a pull from the cigarette casting a burnt orange glow over his face. "Lousy thing, being enemies, I won't get to enjoy it for long." Jude's ears perked. It sounded like a thousand claws were scratching at the underside of the pavement. After a few seconds passed, Jude realized the scratching was not originating from one location, but all around him. As he instantly changed form, the overwhelming stench of sulfur battered his nostrils. His eyes picked up sil-houettes, but could not distinguish between shadows, pavement, and beast.

With a snap of Lucius's fingers, the beasts erupted into flame illuminating the gravity of Jude's situation. He was sur-rounded by 12 hounds that roughly resembled German Shep-herds. They were scaled on every inch of their bodies. The scales were ebony where usual shepherds are black, yet were lava orange where the coat is usually tan. "Always have to be over-dramatic don't you, Lucius?"

Lucius raised his arms to his sides, palms up. "Nah, just enough flare to be stylish." He grinned. "Pun intended." He lowered one arm and waved with the other. "See you later... then again." Lucius vanished.

Jude transitioned from conversation to focusing on the sit-uation at hand. He flexed his paws and lengthened his claws to six inches, a trick he had learned since his battle with Adam and Lucius in New York.

The hound located in front of Jude began creeping for-ward. Molten saliva dripped from its mouth. He heard a quickened pace from behind him. Without looking, Jude cat-apulted his arm behind him with his claws pointing skyward. His claws sank into the hound's neck. The momentum of his arm lifted the beast over his head straight on top of the dog in front of him. Both instantly burst into a cloud of embers.

The hounds on his left and right moved and he barely had enough time to react. He swung his arms up and around claw-ing both dogs through the skull. Jude continued the move-ment and slammed both hounds together in front of him, turning them to ash. As ten and five moved with a rapid pace, he arced his arm with enough force his claws sank into the scales behind another's head and cut clean through. The dog's head thudded to the pavement before melting into and orange puddle. Searing pain shot through Jude's right side. He had been too slow to react to the sixth's movement. The hound jumped and clawed into the right, middle side of Jude's back. It leveraged off of this point and clamped its jaw down over his shoulder. As Jude reached up and dug his claws into the nape of the dog's neck, the rest swarmed. He tore the head away from the neck of the beast and his shoulder. After the head burst into a cloud of smoke and ash, Jude began clawing at the remaining hounds biting and clawing at his body. Slowly, one by one, he defeated the pack. His breathing was labored and heavy, not just from exertion, but also due to massive injuries. A few of the dogs had melted down his side as he dispatched them. His other injuries were bite and claw marks, that stung with excruciating keenness. As he collapsed to the ground with smoldering piles of ashes around him, his vision began to narrow into darkness. The last sight his eyes beheld before his eyes closed to an uncertain future was a winged figure stepping out of the darkness.

# CHAPTER 17

F ather Donovan turned onto the onramp for I-90 heading towards Gary, Indiana. His impending business was not relative to the church. He was meeting a borrower that had called to inform him that he had the money and was willing to meet him in an inconspicuous location.

The Father glanced at the revolver tucked between the driver's seat and the center console. Although, this certain individual seemed civil, he never took any chances.

His thoughts began wondering over the amount of money he was about to be paid. Was it smart to immediately spend money from a client? No. He usually waited for it to be laundered before spending it. That way it made it practically untraceable and he could spend it without concern. Donovan needed a break anyways. As soon as the meeting was finished, he would drive to O'Hare and book the next flight out to The Maldives.

After a few more miles, he began tapping his thumbs and fingers on the steering wheel. Realizing what had been missing, he reached down and pressed the power button on the stereo. The car was instantly flooded with Bon Scott's vocals belting out, "Highway to Hell". Donovan chuckled and shook his head. "Perfect."

He cruised a few miles more, keeping beat on the steering wheel and singing off key. Donovan zoned for a split second until a silhouette appeared ahead of him. As he swerved to miss the man, he was able to see the face of the person that he was on his way to meet. His car hit the wall along the shoulder, the nose of his car turned into the wall, and the car began rolling.

The car came to a stop right-side-up. Donovan's door was pulled open and the seatbelt fell loose like it had been cut. His contact pulled him from the wreckage and pulled him forward so they were face to face. "Hello, Jack. Good to see you." He glanced around. "I don't see a bag." His head started to swim and he rolled his eyes and blinked to clear it. "Jack, does this mean you won't be repaying me tonight?"

"You don't know how right you are, Phillip." The silky voice emanated from the darkness, just beyond his view. "You, on the other hand," A man stepped forward into the light. "...will be repaying plenty."

Phillip Donovan, glanced over to the clean-cut arrival. "Who are you?"

The man grinned. "Don't get too hasty. You'll have the rest of eternity to understand who I am." The man laid his hand on Jack's shoulder. "He's all yours. Enjoy, I know how you prefer to savor the moment."

Jack nodded and began allowing his face to change form.

Donovan's eyes went wide. "God in Heaven!"

The stranger tapped Jack on the shoulder. "Hold up." Jack's face returned to normal. "Oh, Phillip. Don't be calling to him, when you sold your soul to me." He shook his head. "What would the Church say?" He glanced at Jack as he turned to leave. "He's all yours."

As the man turned to leave, Phillip looked back at Jack. His face already had changed back to its reptilian form. Jack spread his serrated row of teeth and, in the snap of them closing, bit clean the front half of Phillip's head. Jack remained motionless and watched the body slump to the ground while twitching with the remaining nerve impulses fading. He spit the contents in his mouth onto the body. His face returned to normal except for his eyes, which allowed him to see in the dark. Before stepping into the darkness, Jack grinned as he glanced down to see a frozen expression of terror on Father Donovan's halved face.

# CHAPTER 18

A dam sat in a coffee shop, taking a little time for himself. Jess was at the apartment with the boys and told him to go unwind. He always thought of how amazing she was as a spouse and mother. Whenever she could see the stress from his work and fighting the beasts of nightmares, she would make him go take some time to decompress from it all.

He sipped his black coffee and watched people passing on the sidewalk, thinking back to how everything had started for him in this entire mess. He had started drinking in excess and staying at the office way too much. Adam smirked as he looked into the liquid in his cup. It scared him, just how much he used to be like Christophe. Adam had no idea how much his father-in-law drank, but he did know that he had always put his career before everything else.

As Adam looked up and back out of the window, a familiar figure skirted by. His eyes followed the figure past the window and saw him enter the shop. Michael sat down across from Adam a little winded. Adam smirked. "Are you okay?" He turned and looked out of the window behind him. "Lucius isn't on your heels, is he?"

Michael's expression was oddly firm. Usually, he would laugh along with the joke, but not this time. "Laugh it up, but I guarantee you that you'll be straight faced soon enough."

Adam sipped from his cup. "Are you sure about that, fly boy? Just wait until Jude gets here. I'll see if he's wanting to get you in stitches."

"Jude is here." Adam looked around then shook his head and shrugged his shoulders. "He's in the hospital." Adam's expression dropped and Michael pointed. "Told you." He sat forward and leaned on the table with his arms. "He was attacked last night in an alley. I got to him just as he passed out. I took him to the hospital and told them not to ask questions. Luckily his body had reverted to human form before we walked through the doors."

Adam sat with his left arm tucked under his right and his right hand grasping his coffee cup. He nodded and looked up at Michael. "Do we know what did it?"

"I arrived just as he was finishing off the last of them, but it was a pack of hell hounds that look eerily similar to German Shepherds. He was surrounded by piles of ash. I have had my fair share of run ins with them over the millennia and am surprised he survived a solo bout with more than a few."

Adam nodded his head and exhaled. "How bad is he?"

Michael leaned back into his chair. "He'll be alright, but it will take a day or two for his body to heal. We have some antidotes that can heal, but his wounds were too great for it to be of any help."

Adam smirked. "Knowing Jude, the nurses will be glad to be rid of him."

Michael nodded. "You do have a point there. Once he's back on his feet and out of the hospital, then we can meet and figure out the plan on how to take this thing down."

Adam took another sip of coffee. "How deep are we in this?"

Michael's brow furrowed then raised. "Considering that we're the only team protecting the world...inconceivably."

Adam downed the rest of his coffee as Michael's eyes widened and became more alert. "So, what kind of monster are we--"

Michael stood, toppling his chair in the process. "Get to Jess and the boys. Now!" Before he finished talking, Adam was at the door.

* * *

Jess got the twins dressed and ready to surprise Christophe at the office. This time, Charlie, fought her more than usual. He sat on the floor throwing a tantrum and Justin sat trying to calm him. "Come on, Charlie. It will be fun. Maybe Grandpa will treat us to food at a new restaurant." He held his jacket up in front of him. Charlie calmed and looked at his coat and then to his brother. "Come on, bub. I know you've got to be hungry."

Charlie nodded and took his jacket from Justin. As he stood to put it on, Jess looked at Justin. "Thank you for your help."

"You're welcome, momma."

"And thank you, Charlie, for getting ready."

She kissed them both on the tops of their heads. Charlie said, "You're welcome, momma. I'm sorry for being such a handful."

"Why did you not want to go visit grandpa Christophe?"

"I do, but I just have a feeling that something is off."

She paused and looked at him with a raised brow. "What do you mean by 'off', sweetie?"

Charlie tilted his head as he contemplated his wording. "I'm not sure how to describe it. It's like, I knew if we left right then, we would have been in a lot of trouble."

Jess grinned nervously. "We'll be fine, honey. I'm here to protect you. I would never let any harm come to the two of you."

Justin grabbed Jess's hand. "We know that momma."

Jess ruffled his hair. "I know you do. Let's go see your grandpa." She escorted the boys over towards the front door. As they neared the door, a caustic odor burned her nostrils with each step. She brushed it off as someone cleaning the hallway with a powerful solvent.

When she reached for the doorknob, Justin noticed a slight orange glow coming from under the door. He tightened his grip as he looked up and saw Jess's hand turning the knob. Jess swung the door inward to find Lucius's beast on the other side. Its frills were extended wider than the door frame and glowed along with its throat and eyes. The monster seemed to hesitate for a second before stepping back and inhaling a deep breath. The twins jumped in front of Jess, attempting to shield her. She grabbed them by their jackets and threw each to the side, brought up her leg to waist height and kicked the door closed. She saw a flash of turquoise wrap around the beast's body. It threw the monster off balance causing its fireball to hit the top of the door frame.

* * *

Adam ran until it felt like he had boiling antifreeze coursing through his body like an engine. He had been five blocks away when he ran into Michael. Michael gave no explanation and Adam would not have waited for one. A million different thoughts were running through his mind. *Were Jess and the kids still alive? What kind of danger were they in? Was someone breaking in? Was the beast after them? Had it already gotten to them?* Each of Adam's footfalls seemed to take an eternity and seemed to never get him any closer. He felt as if he was running in place. He was moving but everything seemed to be standing still.

Adam reached Christophe's apartment building. He barreled around the corner and ran into a man, knocking him to the ground. He glanced over his shoulder, "Terribly sorry, Sir!" Adam turned back just as the approached the front doors. Without breaking his stride, he grabbed the handle of the closest glass door, flung it open, and continued towards the elevators. As Adam approached, he saw a few people waiting around. He knew they had already pressed the button, but he didn't care. His thumb jack hammered the button.

The people standing close by stared at him as he looked at the illuminated floor numbers as they dinged to 1. As the elevator doors opened to a full car of people to unload, Adam looked towards the ceiling and thought, *are they going to be dead by the time you allow me to reach them?* When the last person stepped off the elevator, Adam stepped in and hit the button for Christophe's floor. No one else stepped on. He figured a lot of them thought he was crazy or needed to get where he was going in such a hurry, that he could have the blasted elevator.

Out of habit he motioned to see if anyone wanted to

board. A heavier set woman looked at him. "Thanks. We'll get the next one." Adam nodded as the doors closed obstructing her face and revealing his reflection. His body remained human, but his eyes were orbs of red and gold. As he felt his adrenaline surge and the oncoming change about to happen, he hadn't realized the elevator car seemed to be moving faster than usual. It started slowing to normal three floors below the Penthouse floor.

When the doors opened, he bolted from the elevator and looked towards Christophe's front door. If not for seeing Jude and himself in changed form, he would not have thought it possible. What stood in front of the door was a six-foot-tall beast that resembled a dilophosaurus. Its scaly frills were outstretched. The frills and the inside of its mouth were glowing a lava orange. As Adam lunged towards the beast, he saw the flap of skin shaking and rattling. He heard Jess scream from beyond the doorway. As his momentum propelled him forward, his change accelerated his movement until his body and head were coiled around the animal's body. The door slammed and he felt the flash of heat from the molten fireball emitted from the monster's mouth.

He picked the beast up and flung it down the hallway closer to the glass window at the opposite end. He glanced at the doorway and wall and saw they were on fire. He smothered the flames with his tail and body putting them out. As soon as he saw nothing but tendrils of smoke rising from the wall, he turned to face his adversary. The monster was just getting to its feet and stared down Adam with its macabre umbrella collapsed firmly along its neck.

His mind began running through the ultimate chess game going on with his surroundings. He thought of all the actions and consequences that presented themselves. If he delayed too long, it would be able to catch the entire floor on fire trapping Jess and the kids and taking an untold number of lives with them. From the sheer muscle mass, he felt when throwing it down the hallway mere moments before, he could tell this thing was powerful. Adam also ran through the thought that there was no telling the extent of the beast's abilities and gifts. All he could tell at the moment was that it was powerful and could spit one heck of a spitball. Being left with no alternative, Adam glanced back over his shoulder towards the door as it began to crack open. He slowly worked his way forward, lessening the gap between himself and the creature. When the gap was half the original distance, he paused, making sure his body created a barricade between the beast and his family. Adam towered the front half of his body until it arched like a cane hook along the hallway ceiling.

He closed his eyes for a split-second while weighing the consequences of his decision. His tongue flicked the air and his eyes shot open. He could taste Jessica's fear. Not just for her safety and the twins, but for his safety as well. The boys, having never seen him in this state, were petrified. Yet, there was another entity that he could sense. The beast was giving off its own pheromones and they wreaked of fear, regret, and excitement. It spread its frills and started slowly pulling in air as it began to illuminate from within. Adam gave it no room to follow through. He speared his body forward into his opponent. The momentum sent them careening through the huge window. Adam heard the beast shrieking, shattering glass, Jess's scream, and then nothing but rushing air.

He saw a flash of wings and reverted back to human form just as Michael plucked him out of midair. As they leveled, he looked and saw Lucius and the beast in human form. They were flying away from him and Michael which obscured their faces. At least he now knew that the demon they were fighting was, in fact, human.

# CHAPTER 19

E veryone had been trying to reach Christophe since the incident. The police told Jess they would go check his work to see if he had just stayed at the office. The lead officer informed her they would let her know whether or not he was still there. She nodded and went back to speaking with the building manager.

Since Adam broke the news to Jess two years before, about his ability, they had concocted a plan if anything should hit close to home, that would explain his whereabouts during an event. Almost on cue, Adam came through the door with a few items from the grocery store. He rushed through the door dropping the bags on the floor as he ran. Stepping up to Jess and the Landlord, he threw his arms around his wife. "Oh my gosh, Jess. What happened? Are you and the boys, okay?"

As he pulled away from her, she said, "We're okay. Just a

little shaken is all."

Adam looked around. "Where's Christophe?"

The Landlord chimed in. "No one has heard from him. Jess was just telling me that the police are going to check his office now to see if he's there." Adam nodded towards the man. Adam readjusted his weight onto his left leg. Looking down at Adam's feet the man looked back up at Adam. "What happened to your leg? If you don't mind my asking."

"No, you're perfectly fine. I stepped wrong off a curb on the way back from the store. It should be fine once I am able to sit down and put some ice on it." He grimaced and turned back to Jess. "What happened?"

"It sounds far-fetched, but there was this massive beast that looked like a dinosaur. It spit a ball of fire as another monster tackled it. If it wasn't for the other creature deflecting its aim, the boys and I would, more than likely, be dead."

The Building Manager's brow furrowed. "What kind of beast was the other creature?"

"Do you remember the incident about two years ago in New York with the giant snake and the lion?" The man gave a silent, slow nod. "From the brief flash I saw right before the door slammed, it looked like that giant snake." The man's jaw dropped and hung loose for a few moments. "Are you okay, Sir?"

The man closed his mouth and shook his head to clear the cobwebs. "Yes. Would you be willing to give a statement to the insurance agent tomorrow about this?"

She nodded and smiled. "I would be more than happy to, if you think it will help."

He nodded. "Thank you so much, Jessica." He patted Adam on the shoulder. "And you, get that foot propped and iced."

Adam smiled. "Will do." The man turned and left the apartment inspecting the door and hall once again before heading for the elevator. Adam hobbled over to the bags and went to the kitchen to put away the groceries. Other than a few Firefighters down the hall that were still checking damage and for any remaining hot spots, they were alone. "So, what's the game plan?"

"If you're okay staying with the boys, I think I may go to Dad's office and see if he's there. At minimum, if he isn't, I can see if I can dig up answers to see if he's been there at all today."

"Are you sure it's safe? Whatever this thing is, just about killed you and the boys."

"I should be fine as long as I've got openings to get away or take cover. Here in the apartment however, we were trapped."

Adam nodded as he put a gallon of milk into the refrigerator. "I've got it. Just be careful and keep me posted." He turned and rested his hands on the counter. "Let me know if you need anything."

She leaned across the bar and kissed him. "I will. Be sure to prop that leg up and ice it."

He hobbled around the bar to where she could see his entire body. "Actually," He lifted his pant leg revealing numerous cuts to his leg. "...it's glass and not a twisted ankle." Blood had ran down his sock, dying it red.

She reached over the bar and grabbed the dish towel folded on the counter. "Oh, my word, Adam! Why didn't you say something sooner?" He stopped her hands before they could put pressure on the wounds with the towel. She looked up at him confused. "What?"

"There's still glass in it. If you put pressure on it, it will do more damage." He took her hands in his and started raising her back up to her full height. "I'll be fine. Jude and Michael are supposed to be meeting me here any minute. I'll get them to help me remove the shards. Once they're out the wounds should heal in no time." She gave a short nod. "Go check on Christophe. With that thing coming here, it's hard telling who was the target. The most logical guess would be me, but I wouldn't put it past Lucius to have reasons to go after you, the kids, or Christophe."

"Now, I'm scared."

Adam embraced her. "I know, Sweetheart. It'll all be fine. We will get through this safe and sound. I won't let anything happen to you or the boys."

She pulled back. "That's not what I meant. I'm scared of you, Jude, and Michael being in the same room at the same time. There's no telling what kind of mischief you'll get into with me gone." Adam laughed and kissed her.

"You never fail to make me love you more. With all the stuff we have going on, you still have the strength and sense of humor to give me a hard time." He cupped her cheek in the palm of his hand. "I've got the fort. Go check on Christophe and see if he's okay. If he was the target, then we should tell him about what happened as soon as possible." He kissed her again. "I love you so much, Jessica."

She placed her forehead on his. "I love you too." She pulled away and started towards the door. "I'll message if I find anything out." She turned left outside of the door and headed for the elevator.

\* \* \*

As Jessica neared Christophe's office building her phone

started buzzing from her front pocket. She glanced around to make sure no one was following her or creeping towards her from the shadows. The ID registered unknown. She accepted the call, "Hello? This is Jessica."

"Mrs. Campbell?"

"Yes."

"This is Sergeant Lee from the Chicago PD."

Jessica stutter stepped before stopping. "Were you able to find my father?"

"Yes Ma'am. He's been at work this entire time."

She began walking again, but at a faster pace. "Thank you so much, Sgt. Lee! I'm actually just approaching the building now."

"You're welcome, Mrs. Campbell. Have a great evening."

"Thank you. You do the same, and stay safe."

"Will do, Ma'am."

Jess hung up the phone and placed it back in her pocket. She entered the glass doors at the front of the office building and bee lined for the elevators. *What could he have been up to this evening? Why hadn't he answered his phone? Did he even read his texts?*

The elevator dinged when she arrived at her needed floor, and she stepped off when the doors slid open. She heard yelling from the elevator corridor. As she rounded the corner, she anticipated seeing Shannon sitting behind her desk as usual. Her chair was vacant. Jess noticed Christophe's door was slightly cracked and saw half of Shannon's silhouette just past the door frame. "What the heck were you thinking?" Christophe's voice bellowed through the cracked door.

Jess could hear sobbing in Shannon's retort, "I'm so sorry, Mr. Picard."

"How many times have I told you never to allow Chicago

PD admittance to my office?"

"Countless times, Sir. I just figured you would have wanted to make an exception this time, considering they were here about your well-being and to let you know that Jess and the boys were safe."

"Well, Shannon, once again you were wrong." Jess saw him disappear from behind his desk and reappear in front of Shannon. He leaned against his desk and folded his arms across his chest. "With this deal on the line, why would you think I would make the time to worry about my family's welfare? We've been through this before."

Jess balled her shirt in her fist over her heart and raised her other hand to her mouth.

"Are you hearing yourself? I know you've always held your job to the highest standards. I've even heard you admit, sometimes, higher than your own family, but never over their well-being. Christophe, you have now passed into the realm of madness."

Jess watched as Christophe raised to his full height. She could see his scarlet face. He looked like he would hit Shannon at any moment. He paused, then turned, and walked back to the window facing the cityscape. "It's not like I haven't handled an account like this on my own before." He shrugged his shoulders. "And, now that I have years of experience under my belt, it should be all the easier." Christophe turned and faced Shannon. "Go pack your belongings. You're fired." He sat in his office chair, put his feet up on the desk, and laced his fingers behind his head.

Shannon stood opposite him with determination. "After all these years, you're just going to let it end like that, huh?"

He gave a slight turn of his head towards her and nodded. "Yeah."

Shannon left the office and slammed the door on her way out. She took a deep breath in with her eyes closed and opened them as she exhaled. It was at that moment she noticed Jess standing against the wall, shirt still clenched in her fist and hand still covering her mouth. Her cheeks glistened streaks of tensile. "How much did you hear, Sweetie?"

Jess's hand dropped from her mouth. "Enough to know he's been lying to me for years." Shannon let a single tear fall and waved for Jess to come over to her.

As they embraced halfway across the room, Shannon said, "I'm so sorry, Sweetheart. I wish I could have told you the truth years ago, but he had threatened to fire me if I told you anything."

"In reality this trip was my last effort to see if there was any hope of him putting his family first." She pulled back. Fresh tears streaming down her face. "I feel like such an idiot." Shannon pulled away and started gathering up her belongings.

"You're not an idiot. He's been hiding stuff like that for years. From your mother as well. God rest her."

Jess wiped the tears from her cheek. "Do you have any idea where you'll go or what you'll do?"

Shannon sat down, raised her arms, and dropped her hands to her knees with a smack. "Not a clue, Dear. I'm sure, with my experience, it won't be too difficult to find something."

"If you can't, let Adam or I know and we'll be more than happy to help find you something. Even if it's clear up in New York by us."

Shannon nodded. "Thank you."

Jess paused and breathed a deep breath. "Now, if you'll excuse me, I have some business to attend to."

Shannon cocked her head towards the door. "Go get him." Jess nodded and walked through the door.

As she stepped through the door and clicked it shut behind her, Christophe gave her a blank look. He lowered his feet and turned towards the window. "Please, have a seat."

"I'd prefer to stand, thank you." She leaned back against the door.

"I take it you heard me talking with Shannon over the last few minutes?"

She saw his reflection in the window. "Yes, I did."

"And you're not going to say anything? Just wait for me to talk before giving me short answers?"

She saw his head nod slightly. "That pretty much sums it up."

Jess's voice rose a few decibels. "Why did you fire her?"

Christophe's voice remained flat as he turned to face her and said, "Because, she allowed the police in here. I don't need them snooping or any nosey brats in here snooping as well."

"So, that's all I am to you. A brat that is just a drain on your time and money." She stepped towards his desk awaiting his answer.

He nodded. "Yep." He looked up at her. "Now that it's out in the open, what do you expect to do about it?"

"How dare you? All these years, you lied to me, to Mom! All for what? Money? Greed?" He gave her a straight glare, nodded once. "You're pathetic. I can't believe I came back here thinking there was a shred of hope that you had changed. I'm an idiot for not seeing it sooner." She stepped up to the desk and leaned across closer to her father. "You are the worst type of person imaginable. You lied to your own child for years. I pity you." She slapped his face with enough force to immediately leave a hand shaped welt. "Your daughter and grandchildren were in extreme danger tonight, and you act like it was any other normal day." She turned and headed towards the door. "We'll be moving to a hotel for the remainder of our stay." She turned to face him as she walked out of the door. "I never want to hear from you again." She pulled the door to as she exited with a quiet click.

# CHAPTER 20

**H**arry Brimmer stepped into the storage area of the small arts shop that he operated. Most of the pieces were fakes, but they were so good, no one could tell the difference. He turned to slide a drawer out in the wall unit. A dark shadow appeared in the doorway. Harry paused and then pulled the drawer open to remove a painting.

"Hello, Jack."

A man dressed in a leather brown suit stepped from the shadows. "Hello, Harry." Jack walked further into the light. "I was hoping to startle you …at least a little bit."

Harry looked down at the painting. He looked back up at Jack with a smirk. "Sorry to disappoint." Pivoting on his feet, he carried the painting over to a waist-high table. "Why should I be startled? After all, you are one of our silent investors."

Jack walked the ten feet to where Harry stood. "Uh huh." He looked down at the piece of art facing up at them. "This is beautiful."

"It definitely is, we should be able to get a pretty penny from it."

Jack looked up at Harry. "Is it really worth that much?"

Harry shook his head while picking a frame from the rack next to the table. "No, but the buyer won't know the difference."

Jack nodded and looked back at the piece. "Wow." He placed his hand on the table. "Quite an enterprise you've got going …well …had."

Harry's eyes flickered left for a brief instant to read if Jack showed any sign of amusement. A wisp of a smirk crossed his face. "What do you mean, 'had'?"

"It ends tonight."

Harry laughed. "Funny joke."

Jack leaned closer to the painting. "Did I give any hint that I was joking?" A bead of sweat rolled down Harry's forehead. "You've been late on your payments for far too long."

"Come on, Jack. I can have the money for you in a couple of days."

"It's too late for excuses and extensions." Jack's hand lifted looking human, except an extended reptilian index finger. With a blurred flick of his wrist, his claw sliced through Harry's neck as easy as air.

Harry's eyes widened. At seeing the painting spattered red, he raised his hands to his throat. He coughed, spraying a mist across the artwork from his lacerated neck. A moment later, his body thudded to the floor.

Jack leaned over the painting. "Now it's even more beautiful." He stepped over Harry's twitching body and left the shop.

# CHAPTER 21

K nowing that Michael and Jude would be arriving soon, Adam started a fresh pot of coffee. He got into the cabinet and set out three cups. Growing bored waiting, his footsteps lead him down the hallway to check on the boys again. He stood by the door pondering how precious they were to him.

Adam heard a soft opening and closing of the apartment door. He gently pulled the door closed to so their discussion would not disturb the twins. Upon entering the living room, he found Jude and Michael, in regular human clothes, standing in the entryway, staring at the damage. Jude was massaging his right shoulder.

They turned to face him. The two smiled as he stepped up to them. Adam, reached out and shook Jude's hand. "It's about time you two showed up." He smirked at Jude as he shook Michael's hand. "What happened to your shoulder?"

He massaged deeper into his shoulder and grimaced. "Blasted, Hell Hound. In reality, 12 of them."

Michael stepped forward and pulled Jude's shirt back to inspect the wound. He nodded as to affirm that its healing looked to be on track. "Won't take too much longer to heal, but the painful ache will probably linger for quite some time."

Jude looked over his shoulder and nodded. "Thanks."

Adam turned and headed towards the kitchen. "Does coffee sound good to either of you?"

Michael and Jude turned to follow him. They said in unison, "I could go for a cup."

They both turned to glance at Michael. With a huff he threw up his hands. "I had no idea he was going to say it too. Would I lie?" Jude and Adam looked back at each other and shook their heads as they finished walking to fill their cups. As Michael poured his cup, he looked at Adam. "How's the leg?"

Adam raised his pant leg to inspect his wounds. "It still has glass in it and burns every time I move." Michael stepped forward to inspect it. He took a small vile from his pocket, and dropped a single drop on each wound. Tiny masses began surfacing from Adam's wounds and clinked on the floor. The crimson-colored wounds began to turn pink and close as they watched. "What is that?"

Michael stood up and said, "An ointment made from Angel urine."

Adam reached for something to wipe his leg. "That's disgusting!"

Jude's brow furrowed. "That's just nasty."

Michael smirked and started laughing as he placed his hand on Adam's shoulder. "Easy. Do you believe everything

I tell you?" He held up the vile. "It's from a celestial creek."

Jude laughed as Adam raised his brow and asked, "You sure about that?"

Michael nodded. "Adam, about earlier, did the man Lucius carry away look familiar?"

Adam lowered his pant leg and leaned back against the counter. He stared at the floor for what seemed like an eternity before shaking his head. "I can't say that he did. I've been trying to replay every instant from earlier to see if there was a little glimpse or even a reflection that I could have picked up. I didn't get any kind of look at the person's face."

Michael lowered his head and thought for a moment. "So, there was absolutely nothing?"

Jude leaned back against the counter and crossed his arms with the coffee cup still in one hand. Adam looked into Michael's eyes. "There was a moment, before I lunged and we both went out the window, that the monster hesitated. It was only a split second, but it still slowed just a bit."

Michael looked at Jude and saw his intense dead stare at Adam. Michael turned back to Adam and asked with a furrowed brow, "What changed?"

Adam's brow lowered. "Jess stepped out into the hallway."

Michael paused and looked as if he was listening. "Adam, pack your family's belongings and take them and the boys to the nearest hotel. We'll have someone watch over the boys while they're there. After you drop them off, meet us by Christophe's office building."

Adam's face paled. "What's wrong?"

"All they told me was that Jess was in trouble."

"Why is this all centering around Jessica?"

Jude set his cup down on the counter. "I don't know but

the longer we stay the longer we're not there to protect her." Adam nodded and ran into the bedroom as Michael and Jude headed for the door.

Jude glanced at Michael as they started running down the hallway. "Air or on foot."

Michael smiled at Jude. "The window's already open. Why waste a great exit?" They both dove out of the broken window into the rising glow of the street below.

# CHAPTER 22

J essica entered the lobby from the elevator. She kept it all together as she slowly walked through the big glass doors out onto the busy sidewalk. It was at times like these that made her grateful she had such a strong will. She had walked half a block when she saw an alley and stepped into it. Jess knew from living in New York City, that an alley was not a place a person sought solitude after dark. She leaned against the wall in shadow so she wouldn't be seen from the sidewalk or street.

In the darkness, her will broke and she let the torrent flow. If anyone were brave enough to attack her at this point, it would have been the last mistake they ever made. Her face contorted in a strangled silent anguish. Years of frustration, anger, sadness, disappointment, and a plethora of other feelings that accompanied the waterfalls flowing down her cheeks. Her chest hurt from holding back the sobs that were wracking her organs.

*What made me believe he could change? Why would I think things could be different from what they were when I was little? He has no remorse for lost time. Does he even have an iota of feeling for me?*

Hearing more footsteps clacking on the sidewalk just outside the alley, she looked up to see people laughing and enjoying each other's company as they walked. It looked to be a family with G=grandparents, children, and grandchildren.

*Why can't I experience happiness like that? Am I cursed to not have a normal family?*

She then glanced at the faces of the children. Her heart skipped a beat and she realized she already had all she needed.

*What am I doing? Everything I need in a family, I already have. I'm through holding out hope that he could change. I will redirect my love, hope, and affection whole heartedly towards Adam and the boys.*

She straightened up to head back to Christophe's apartment when a door at the back of the alley flew open. Jess leaned back against the wall. She could see two shadows flying out of the door and stood close enough to a light to illuminate their faces. She recognized both. The man facing her was her father and the other was Roman. She could see the vein pulsing out of his forehead, which was never a good sign. Every time that vein became visible, it meant he was about to have an epic meltdown. "When am I going to get what you promised?"

Roman responded with a silky, baritone voice, "Patience. You'll get what you bargained for."

"What about my family? I thought you'd said that would

be part of the deal."

"I promise you, by the end of this, you will earn her love again. The wealth and power will come soon enough as well. You just have to do a little bit more before you receive them."

"It's not soon enough! We made a deal and you need to stand by it in a timely manner! Why must I keep waiting?" Jessica could tell his voice was taking on more of a growl.

Roman stepped up to him. "You should know better than to call me out on anything." He began taking a cigarette from its box and tapped the filter onto the pack. "Has the gift I've given you made you stupid?"

Christophe calmed. "No."

Roman lifted the cigarette to his mouth and lit it. "You do remember that you were almost bankrupt and pathetic when we made our deal, don't you?"

He lowered his head and nodded. "Yes."

Jess still watched from the shadows, remembering and contemplating everything she was seeing. *Who the heck is this guy? He has completely decimated his anger in just moments.*

Roman stepped forward and blew smoke into Christophe's face. "Now here is what's going to happen. You're going to use that anger, and go out" He pointed with his thumb over his shoulder. "…on the streets and start wreaking havoc."

Christophe's brow furrowed. "What do you mean?"

"What I mean is, go out on those streets, tear stuff up, kill people, and let your anger be in control." He stepped away from him and punched him across the face. Christophe's knees shook, then buckled. "You're still here? Go!"

The form that rose, was one she had hoped she wouldn't see again. Unfortunately, this was the second time she was seeing it in a single day. Her heart dropped at the realization.

*Daddy, what have you done? It's as if you've made a deal with the devil himself. Why couldn't you just be happy with us? What is so important about money and power?*

She was so focused on what was happening deep within the alley that she didn't see a man step up in front of her. Her mind quickly realized what was happening as the man's hand wrapped around her throat. Her tears rolled down her neck and over his fingers. "Give me everything you've got!" He looked up and down her body and then into her eyes as he grinned. "And, I do mean everything."

As Jessica had been too distracted to see the man approach, her attacker was too distracted in his pursuits to notice the six-foot lizard at the back of the alley. As Christophe flew by the two on his way to the street, the man's eyes went wide. All Jess felt was a puff of air on her face before a wet mist covered her face and the man's head fell from his body at her feet.

Roman stood in the shadows of the alley, grinning, and looking on with red irises.

# CHAPTER 23

A dam entered the hotel and approached the front desk pushing a cart loaded with their luggage, Justin, and Charlie. He stopped the cart at the desk, where a young woman looked up and greeted him.

"Good evening, Sir. How may I help you?"

Adam's mouth gave a faint rise at its corners. "Hi. I was told I could bring my boys here." The girl raised an eyebrow. "A friend said that they and everything else would be taken care of."

The lady nodded. "And, what's your name, Sir?"

"Yes, it's Adam Campbell. My friend's name is Michael." He watched as she punched the information into her computer. Her expression flattened as she concentrated on the displayed list on the monitor.

She smiled as she looked up at him. "Yes, sir, Mr. Campbell. Everything is certainly squared away."

She grabbed the room keys and swiped them to activate them. She slid the keys across the desk to him. The lady walked into the office and exited through a side door into the lobby and walked up to Adam. "If you would please follow me; I will show you to your suite." She grabbed a corner bar of the bellman cart and started maneuvering it as if it, and its cargo, weighed a couple pounds. She led the way to the elevators and pressed the up button.

Adam looked at her reflection in the elevator doors as she watched the numbers counting down to one. "What's your name, ma'am?"

Her reflection glanced at him. "My name's Daphne. My apologies for not telling you sooner."

Adam smiled as the bell on the elevator chimed and the doors parted. "That's quite all right." She pulled the cart into the elevator car and leaned against the wall after hitting the button for the top floor.

Adam watched the boys for a few seconds and glanced at Daphne, to find her, looking at the twins as well. "They're adorable. You and Jess are so blessed."

"Thank you, Daphne. We sure ar—How do you—"

She stood up and began walking forward as the car stopped and the tone sounded. Her motion was fluid as she stepped through the doors as they opened, pulling the cart with her. As she entered the elevator corridor, she took a left followed by a right once in the main hallway. Adam continued to follow her until she stopped by a door at the end of the hall. She slid a key into the door and pulled the cart into the suite. As Adam crossed the threshold, he pursed his lips and raised his eyebrows. "This place is almost as large as Christophe's penthouse."

"That it is, Adam, but you need to go." She turned and

looked into his eyes with pearl irises and pupils. "You are needed elsewhere."

Adam gave a single nod and then looked to his sons. "They will be fine. They do have the protection of Heaven on their side."

Adam looked back to Daphne. "Thank you. If they wake while I'm gone, tell them I love them."

Daphne closed her eyes and bowed her head. Adam started for the door.

# CHAPTER 24

J ess sat on the ground with her back against the alley wall. She wasn't sure how much time had passed since her father had changed form and ran by while exiting the alley. Her thoughts had been a torrent of jumbled confusion since witnessing the exchange between Roman and Christophe. The eyes from the severed head, resting on the ground, between her feet, judged her. She took in a deep breath and stood.

She heard the screams, coming from the street, dying in the distance. Knowing her father was getting farther from her reach, she was unsure of what she could do to save whoever she could, but she would do anything in her power to stop his rampage. She kicked the head into the wall facing her and left the alley to follow the screams.

As she stepped out of the alley and turned right to follow

the sounds of panic, she saw bodies littering the pavement. Christophe had not heeded age nor gender. Jess covered her mouth to stifle the screams rising from her core. As she ran towards her father, she ran past bodies of elderly couples holding hands and children entombed in parents' arms; Crimson cascaded down their bodies and pooled on the concrete. The tears flowed and dripped onto her shirt and coat as she ran.

Jess looked ahead and could see people running towards her. Their complexions were white with wide eyes. The sounds of panic grew louder with every footfall. She came within view of Christophe, just as he was crunching through a man's skull and throwing him into the side of an adjacent building. The man's body dropped to the ground as Jess finally came within earshot of her father. He paused and sniffed the air in search of something. He lowered his head and slowly turned to look into her eyes.

As Christophe began taking slow steps towards Jessica, his frills expanded, and his throat and frills began to glow. She could tell his overall size had increased since their earlier meeting at the apartment. He was easily 20 feet long from nose to tail. He continued to stalk forward. Christophe sucked in a lungful of air, when he was about 10 yards from her. Jess ducked behind a parked work van just as he spit a stream of molten sludge. She could smell and hear the metal melting under the extreme heat. Jess, staying low, darted for cover beside the next vehicle. She peaked over the hood to keep her sight on Christophe. He was still approaching at a slow pace and she could see that he was already building for another incendiary burst.

She ducked for cover and moved to the rear of the car and continued to watch Christophe through the windows.

Christophe's frills fluttered as he prepared to let loose with another attempt to char Jessica from existence. Jessica started to lean back on her heals, preparing to seek cover behind the next vehicle, when a figure flew in behind the monster. Jess noticed the figure was carrying another that it dropped behind Christophe. She immediately recognized the figure to be Jude in his lion form. The other man flipped in mid-air bringing a shield to his front, tucked his wings behind his back, and held the shield between himself and the monster.

Christophe's attack erupted from his throat. The rim of the man's shield began to glow and his figure darkened. The force of the attack was so strong is began pushing him backwards, yet he never faltered. He tightened into himself to lower his center of gravity and angled his shield to deflect the stream into the car across the street from Jessica.

Without turning to look at her he yelled, "Get out of here, Jessica! Get to safety! Adam has taken the boys to a hotel! They'll be safe there!"

Her brow furrowed as she glanced at Christophe before fleeing. The tears flowed as she headed away from the scene. She had just started wondering which hotel she needed to go to, when an inner voice told her the name of the hotel.

# CHAPTER 25

Once Jessica was a safe enough distance away, Jude made his move while Christophe was still in the middle of his attack on Michael. He sprung straight up into the air and extended his claws during his decent. As soon as his feet connected with scales, he sank his claws deep into Christophe's neck. The scaled beast clipped off his attack and slammed his frills closed on Jude's hands, trapping them in place. Jude's eyes widened as he saw the scaled head and neck begin to rotate. He tried to flex his fingers to do some damage to the creature and see if it would distract the beast and buy him time. Christophe's head had turned a complete 180 degrees and was looking Jude directly in the eyes.

Jude looked past the beast's head hoping that Michael would jump into action. Michael peaked over the edge of his shield. As he looked and saw the predicament that Jude was in, he failed to realize the monster was mutating once again. The change was subtle, but one Michael should have seen. Its arms grew and thickened from short, dual clawed twigs to human-like, 10-digit appendages.

As Jude struggled to free his claws from the beast's neck, he felt a searing sensation around his own neck. A split second later, he realized it wasn't just stinging, but tightening. Seeing the tip of Christophe's tail wrapped around Jude's neck, Michael charged forward and drew his sword. As Michael slid under Christophe like a baseball player sliding into base, he sliced along the beast's chest and stomach. Christophe let out a shriek while extending his frills and turning his head to look underneath his body. His tail released from around Jude's neck as he grabbed one of Michael's wings.

With the pressure off his neck, Jude withdrew his claws from Christophe's throat and jumped down from his back. He massaged his nape and quickly pulled his hand away as the acid residue started burning his paw pads. With the park directly behind them, Jude ran over and rinsed his neck off in the fountain. He wondered what had caused the beast to release its hold on him.

Jude's eyes began frantically scanning the area as he rushed back to where the battle was taking place. He realized he hadn't seen Michael as he jumped down from the scaly hide of the monster. His brows shot up towards his mane and his feet started covering ground faster when he saw a glimpse of the beast with a wing in each hand. Michael was trapped under the monster and taking a heck of a beating. As Michael's wings were held, the creature was stomping up and down his body.

Jude ran up behind the beast just as it landed a kick to Michael's head that caused it to bounce off the pavement. His claws were glowing as he pulled both arms back and slammed them shut driving his claws into the base of the monster's tail. It let out a deafening scream as it released its hold on Michael's wings and turned its head to face Jude. As Michael slowly rolled over and crawled out from under the monster, Jude began pulling and swinging the beast to get it off balance. He watched the beasts head and felt for any flexing in its tail to judge how it would move next.

Christophe was one step ahead of Jude. He lashed Jude's back with his tail knowing it would cause Jude to gasp in pain. As soon as Jude exhaled with the reaction, Christophe lashed his tail around Jude's neck once again. He could feel the weakening in Jude's claws right before they lost purchase of his tail. Jude reached up and began trying to claw at the scaled noose around his neck. He could smell his fur, skin, and claws deteriorating from the acid. His peripheral vision began to go black as oxygen deprivation drew him closer to passing out. Feeling Jude's body beginning to go slack, Christophe dropped him to the pavement and jumped towards the closest ally entrance.

Jude placed his paws on his knees and started pulling in deep, slow breathes. After a taking a few, his vision began to widen, and his thoughts cleared. He looked up to see the monster spring-boarding from wall to wall heading towards the rooftops. Jude took a deep breath and shook his head as he ran towards the alley. As he approached, he leapt onto a dumpster and started his way up, mimicking the beast's movements. As Christophe reached the rooftop, he gripped the edge with his hands to pull himself up. He saw a blur fly in from the street as he felt Jude's claws find purchase in the flesh of his tail. Christophe screamed and looked down to see

Jude hanging from just below the base of his tail. His tail began to rise to whip around Jude's neck. He saw a glint of wings and steel. Michael flew through and sliced through Christophe's tail severing it from his body. In a fluid motion he made a midair U-turn and flew back slashing the beast's fingers to the bone.

He planted his feet into the side of the building. Bending his knees, he launched himself off the building, catapulting Christophe with him. Jude quickly tucked into a tight somersault pattern trapping Christophe in its momentum. When Jude was 15 feet from the pavement, he used the energy built during the fall to body slam the monster on top of a parked van. The vehicle exploded in a plume of crystalline shards and particles. Jude landed at the beast's feet and launched over Christophe to slow his kinetic movement to a stop in the middle of the street.

Jude turned and faced Christophe as Michael flew in and landed next to him. Michael placed his hand on Jude's shoulder. "Are you okay?"

Jude looked up at Michael and nodded. "I'm fantastic. Where the heck were you?"

"Giving my body time to recoup and my head to stop spinning." He removed his hand from Jude's shoulder and placed it to his head. "Still getting there." Michael looked at Christophe. "What's that smell?"

"That would probably be me. His tail secretes an acid that's been wreaking havoc with my neck and hands." Michael looked up and then realized Jude had wisps of smoke rising from his neck. Jude turned. "I'll be back. I'm going to go rinse my neck and hands in the fountain again to neutralize it."

Christophe started to inhale a deep breath through his

nostrils. As Jude walked back up to Michael's side, his movement was so subtle that neither of them noticed. Jude looked at Christophe. "So, what are we going to do with him?"

"Not sure. I'll have to check with the boss to see what's going to become of him."

Jude chuckled. "Do you have a group coming to pick him up, or do you plan on lifting him yourself?"

Michael laughed. "No, I've got—"

A blast erupted from Christophe as a long turquoise body fell between them and the beast. A hissing scream bellowed from Adam as a black glob of tar-like material slammed into his side. He pivoted his head and neck to bite into the monster's neck. Adam lifted him into the air, arched his neck back, and flung Christophe 300 feet down the street scattering and crushing a row of cars.

He looked down at Michael and Jude. Michael looked up to him. "What took you so long? Did you have to sing them a lullaby?" He noticed Adam wince. He jumped to the other side of Adam's body to inspect the wound. Michael saw that it was smoking and could feel the heat coming from the black cavity burned into Adam's side. "Are you okay?" Adam slithered his head down so his eyes were level with Michael's and nodded. Michael patted Adam's snout.

They all turned to face Christophe, ready for another round. They all moved forward as he rose to his feet from the wreckage and stood in the middle of the street to face them. Christophe extended his frills and let out a tremendous roar that the trio felt from 100 yards away. He then began pacing in a figure eight pattern eyeing them the entire time.

When they were about 50 yards from the beast, Lucius flew in from behind them with a sword in his hand. He sent a torrent of flames towards Michael and Adam, surrounding them in a blazing fog. As he flew over, he slashed deep into Jude's back collapsing him to his knees. Jude looked up in time to see the beast back in human form, facing away from them as Lucius grabbed him under the arms and flew away.

Jude noticed Lucius, this time, looked more like Michael in form. His hair was long and dark; his armor was silver and black; and his wings were pitch black. The flames died down and the three watched Lucius and his pawn disappear into the distance while wincing. Jude stood with blood running down his leg and pooling onto the pavement. Jude asked, "Are you two all right?" He looked at them for their response.

Michael grimaced as he nodded. "Yeah."

Jude looked to Adam. "Adam?"

The red marbled eyes blinked separately just before his giant turquoise and white head gave a single, shaky nod. Jude looked back towards the distance where the two had disappeared. "Was that his original form?"

Michael nodded again. "Pretty much…but the color of his armor was more vibrant than mine. It consisted of gold and silver. He was the most beautiful of our host."

Jude grinned as he rotated his shoulder and touched it with his other hand. "So, I've heard."

Michael looked at Jude inspecting his shoulder. "Don't worry. Help will meet us soon enough. Let's get to a rooftop and out of view of the public. The press should have been scouring the area by now. Luckily, we've had help with keeping them at bay for the time being. Do not revert to human form, either of you. If you do, then it's possible the damage will be more severe and harder to heal. Your bodies have started the healing process already, albeit slow, they're still working on it."

# CHAPTER 26

On the hotel rooftop, 30 minutes later, the three sat waiting for the help that Michael had promised. Jude's bleeding had slowed and some of the char had flaked off from Adam's scales.

Jude looked at Adam and then to Michael. "I hope this help of yours gets here soon. With this acute sense of smell in this form," He looked up at Adam and smiled a serrated grin. "I've got the strangest craving for fried rattlesnake."

Michael laughed as Adam drew his head and neck back, bared his teeth, and hissed. Jude held up his paws. "I can't help it. You smell delicious."

Michael laughed so hard he had tears rolling down his cheeks, when the door to the roof was opened a few moments later. All three snapped their attention to the void waiting to see what stepped out. Michael wiped his cheeks and said,

"There's no reason to be shy. Come on out and stop being self-conscious." Adam and Jude both looked at Michael, then directed their attention back toward the void. A silhouette began to take shape in the door frame. It had pointed ears and a little muzzle. As it stepped out from the shadows, they saw an oversized red panda that stood four feet tall, on all fours, and green where it should have been red.

Jude looked at Adam and then they redirected their gaze to the creature creeping up to them. It inched along until it stood at Michael's feet. The three watched as it looked at Michael and then to Adam and Jude. When it returned its eyes to Michael, he said, "Jude needs more immediate attention. Adam's wounds are cauterized." He kept his eyes on the white and green mass standing in front of him. Reading Jude's mind, he said, "Jude, kneel in front of me, facing me."

The creature stepped back to give Jude space. He took a knee facing Michael grinning as he looked into Michael's eyes. Adam watched as the creature went to work. It opened its mouth and began slowly, exhaling towards Jude's open wound. An emerald green mist emanated from its open mouth and started to drift towards Jude's lacerated flesh, seeping into the open wounds and disappearing. Jude's mouth stretched into a grin. "It's cute. Is this going to be our new mascot?"

Adam's head jerked backwards as the creature's fur turned radiant orange and shot a cone of flame from its mouth for a split second, scorching Jude's open wound for a second. He jumped up screaming, and yelling. "Okay, okay! I get the point. I'm sorry!"

Michael and Adam were laughing. Michael said, "You should know by now not to underestimate anything." His expression flattened. "Now, kneel back down and let them finish."

"Cooking me, or patching me up?" He knelt and the creature began again.

"Little do the two of you know, this addition will be a necessity the next skirmish we have with that beast."

Jude looked at the roof surface at his feet. "Have either of you figured out the beast's identity?" He looked up at Michael, who shook his head. He then looked at Adam, who shook his head while it was lowered causing it to look like a giant, scaled pendulum.

Jude looked back to Michael. "Are there any ideas from our celestial contacts?"

Michael took out his sword and placed the tip on the roof. He began twirling it. "Not a word. For the most part, they've been quiet."

Jude lowered one brow. "What do you mean, 'for the most part'?"

"All that I've been told was that this fight would hit us harder than any of our previous fights. I was told that we would understand when the time was right."

Jude smirked and shook his head. "Not much for giving us any knowledge ahead of time. Are they?"

Michael stopped twirling the sword and looked at Jude with the handle hiding his nose. "I think there is a good reason why they don't want us to know." Jude and Adam traded glances and then looked back at Michael. "I think that if we knew the identity of what we've been fighting, we would refrain from fighting it to our full potential."

Jude and Adam directed their gazes downward with furrowed brows. The panda poked its head out from around Jude and looked at Michael. Michael looked at Jude. "How's the shoulder feel?"

Jude shrugged and rotated his shoulder. He touched it to

find no wound and fur covered skin. "How in the heck did they do that?"

Michael raised his hands out to the sides of his sword, palms up. The sword stood balanced on its tip. "They have a gift." Jude and Adam's jaws fell open as Michael grabbed his sword once again and started twirling it. "And so was that."

Jude turned and started petting under the creature's lower jaw. "Thanks, little guy." The creature jolted back and bit Jude's finger. He pulled his hand away dripping blood. "What the heck?"

Michael said through raking laughter, "You made it angry. Adam, you're up." Jude stood and moved back over to his original location. Adam slithered over to allow the red panda to start the healing process on his smoldering wound.

Jude looked at the creature and asked, "So, do they have a name?"

"Her name is Shannon."

"Well, no wonder why she bit me. Is she going to show us her human form any time soon?" Jude leaned forward, grinning. Shannon paused her healing, turned towards Jude, growled with a snarling lip, and returned to her work on Adam.

"Quit flirting, Jude." Jude looked at Michael. "She's not your type anyway."

"I have a type? How'd you know?"

"I've watched you from before you were born. I know you have a type more than you know, but...on to more important matters. You two will be coming with me for a short time."

Both Jude and Adam looked at each other, then back to Michael. "How long will we be gone?"

"Probably just a couple of days. I'll explain more when we get there."

Adam asked, "Are we leaving immediately, or do we have a day or two to get things in order?"

"I can give you a couple days to get everything in order. We'll literally be gone for maybe two or three days."

Adam shook his head. "I can guarantee you, that Jess is not going to like this one bit."

Michael stopped twirling his sword and leaned the handle back against his shoulder. "You must have faith, Adam. I'm sure she will understand, given the circumstances."

He closed his eyes and lowered his scaled head. "I hope you're right. Is it going to be the three of us?"

Michael shook his head. "No. It will only be you and Jude making the trip with me." Shannon finished her work on Adam and stepped back. "You two go ahead and do what you've got to do to prepare before we leave." They both nodded and turned to leave.

Jude knelt in front of Shannon. "In all sincerity, thank you. You have been a great help." He stood and walked through the door she had used to access the roof.

Adam nodded as he slithered by her. "Thank you for your help, Shannon. I look forward to working with you more in the future." He slithered towards the door and went headfirst through the opening. His body transformed as sections of his body entered the shadows, until a human outline remained and walked down the stairs.

Shannon transformed into her human self after they were both out of sight. Michael walked up and placed his cloak around her naked figure. He waited a few seconds and then removed it from her now clothed form. "Thank you. They are a rather cheeky pair, aren't they?"

Michael looked towards the open door. "Yes, they are. I have grown rather fond of the both of them." He looked back to her. "You will be all right here for a couple of days, won't you?"

She took a deep breath in and nodded. "I should be. How much of a threat is that monster going to be?"

Michael looked up into the distance past her head. He pursed his lips. "I don't think it will be much of a threat with the amount of damage Jude and Adam were able to do. It will at least take a few days for it to heal up to where it's back to fighting strength."

"But, look how quickly I was able to heal Jude and Adam. Surely, it won't take that long for Lucius's demons to heal the beast."

"Severed limbs take longer to heal than burns and lacerations." He looked into her eyes. "Have faith. We'll make it through this. In the meantime, look after the family and let me know if any trouble arises."

She nodded as Michael walked to the edge of the building and stood on the ledge. "Take care of those two."

He grinned and said, "I always do my best." He dropped from the edge of the roof and a second later flew back up above the edge a couple buildings over.

# CHAPTER 27

T he following morning, Adam was up, drinking coffee, and looking out of the window when Jess walked into the kitchen of the hotel suite. Watching her reflection in the window, he said, "Good morning, babe. How'd you sleep?"

She poured a cup of coffee. "Not that great. I tossed and turned most of the night." She walked over and sat down next to Adam. "I've just had so much on my mind lately with the attack and everything going on with my father." She took a sip from her cup and then stared at the dancing reflection on the black surface after she lowered the cup to her lap. "I don't know what's come over him. I mean, he's always been like this, but he seems worse than usual."

Adam placed his hand on her forearm. "I'm sorry that he wasn't a better father. Is there anything I can do to help?"

She shook her head as a tear rolled down her cheek. "No. I just have to get past this. My therapist will have a field day with this trauma." Adam winced as he pulled his hand back and took another sip of his coffee. Jess watched his movements with concern. "Are you okay?"

"Yeah. I got a little banged up in the scuffle last night."

She looked up at Adam. "What do you mean, 'a little banged up'?"

"I shielded Jude and Michael from an attack last night and took a hit to my side." He placed his hand along the side of his ribcage closest to her. "It's not that big."

She reached over and started lifting up his shirt to inspect. "You're grimacing quite a bit." The hem of his shirt rose over the top of the wound revealing it to her. Although it was healed, the scar was about the diameter of small hub cap. "Not that big huh?" She lowered his shirt.

"It was worse. I started healing immediately. At least all the burns from the beast's attack healed before Shannon worked on that wound." He looked into her eyes and could see her confusion and reaching for something to say. "She is one of our new allies and has healing capabilities."

"Is that the Shannon from my father's office?"

He shrugged. "I have no idea. She was in her animal form the entire time. We have never set eyes on her human face." He took a sip of coffee. "It could be, or it could be another Shannon entirely. After all, Chicago is a big city."

"So, you were never alone with her?" Jess' mouth stretched into a grin.

He turned and faced her. "Get that thought out of your head, right now. I have never once thought of another woman, since we've been together. I have always been faithful to you, even when I struggled with drinking."

124

She nodded and leaned in to kiss him. "Touchy, are we? I know you wouldn't. I was only joking and, in all honesty, I'm more scared of losing you to this monster than another woman."

"As long as I'm breathing, you won't." He caressed her face. "I do have to go away for a couple of days."

"Where to?"

He raised his brow and shook his head. "I don't know. Michael never told us. He just gave us a couple days to get everything together."

She nodded and turned to face out of the window again. "I understand."

"I know it will take you away from Christophe for that time, but I would feel more comfortable if you and the boys returned to New York, while I'm gone."

"I wish we were safer here. You don't think since we're in the hotel we'd be safe, do you?"

"The beast already found where you and the kids were. I don't know how it found you, but I know it did.'

She took a sip of her coffee and gave a stiff nod of her head. "Like you said, 'it's a big city'. Maybe, it was just a random coincidence that it came to where the boys and I were."

"Maybe. Or it could have been sent by Lucius as a message to Michael, Jude, and I. All I know is, if you stay here, you're closer to danger. Back in New York, you will have the mileage between you to keep you safe."

Jess let out a long sigh. "If I must, I must. You do make a great point about the distance, but I would rather be close to you. Although, I am not happy with the decision."

Adam nodded. "I understand. I will take the three of you to the airport and see you off tomorrow."

"Can I, at least, go say goodbye to my father before we

leave?"

Adam shook his head. "I don't think that would be such a great idea. With that thing still on the loose, I would feel more comfortable if you just phoned him or sent a text to let him know you were heading home."

She exploded out of the chair. "So, you're going to keep me from seeing him before heading out?" She turned to face him; her face beginning to turn red. "That's just great! I know he isn't the best father, but he's still my father. What if there's a chance for him to change his ways?"

Adam nodded. "I really hope there is a chance for him to change his behavior. I know he hasn't been the best father and I'm sorry. I still would feel more comfortable if you would call or text him. The less anyone is on the streets the better."

Jess shook her head and stormed out of the room. A few minutes later she reentered the living area of the suite fully dressed and headed towards the door. "I'm not a child and won't be told what I can and cannot do, Adam." She pushed down the door handle and pulled the suite door open. "I'll be back shortly. If anything comes up, I'll call or text you. I love you."

Adam knew that determined look in her eyes and that there was no reasoning with her when Jess was in this type of mood. "I love you too."

# Chapter 28

As Jess stepped off the elevator and started walking towards Christophe's office, she could feel a darkness looming throughout the floor. As she maneuvered through the corridor, she could hear voices speaking. There were two men speaking, one of which was Christophe. She slowly approached and listened in on the conversation. On the other side of the door, Christophe stood pacing as Lucius sat in a chair in front of Christophe's desk.

Lucius's hands were laced at the fingers in front of his mouth. He looked from Christophe to the floor and smiled. "Where do your loyalties lie?"

Christophe stopped and looked in his direction. His brow furrowed. "I proved that didn't I? I cut the ties as you requested."

"Are you sure? Your daughter is no longer in the picture

and you've completely severed your bond with her?"

His eyes squinted as he nodded his head. "She ran off right before my last skirmish with those beasts and that annoying angel." He dropped down into his office chair and leaned back. "Who is he anyways? He can't be any high-ranking angel with how easily he took a beating." A slight grin stretched the corners of his mouth.

Lucius leaned back in the chair and rested his face on his right hand. "Actually," He grinned. "He is non-other than the Arch Angel, Michael."

Christophe's expression flattened as he sat forward in his chair. "You mean to tell me, that I trounced one of the highest-ranking angels?"

Lucius nodded.

"Isn't Michael, the Angel of death?"

Lucius lit a cigarette and let the smoke rise between his pointed teeth. "The one and only. He is immature, but don't let your guard down around him." His grin vanished. "When it comes down to it, he is not one with which to mettle."

"He didn't seem that strong the other night."

"There could have been a number of factors that added to him taking that beating. Being in the human world can sometimes be draining, but I'd be willing to bet he was just buying time for his companions."

Christophe nodded and looked down at his desktop for an instant before raising his eyes to meet Lucius's. "Is there a chance they know who I am?"

"Michael, I'm sure of it, but I'm pretty sure he has yet to tell the others."

Christophe stood and looked out of his office window at the city below. "Who are the two beasts who attacked me? Do you know that much?"

"Yes," His smile stretched so wide that the corners of his mouth were above his eyes and his voice took on a tone unlike any human vocalization. "I do."

Christophe shivered as he looked at the demonic reflection in the window. "And?"

"The lion is someone you have not met. The snake is someone you know all too well. The identity of the snake is Adam Campbell."

Christophe turned; the color drained from his face. "Adam Campbell?" Lucius nodded. "My son-in-law?"

"The very one."

Christophe sat back down in his chair. "I wonder if Jess knows."

"Why don't you ask her." He pointed an elongated finger towards the door. "She's been listening in on this entire conversation."

Christophe flew out of his chair and to the door. He flung it open so fast the door handle lodged into the wall to reveal Jess leaning backwards with saucer sized eyes. He grabbed her arm and flung her into the room. Lucius stood and started pacing around the two almost laughing at the turn of events. "What are you doing here?"

"I'm getting ready to head back to New York and wanted to give you one last chance to see if there was any chance left of you changing."

Lucius inhaled deeply of her scent. "Oh Christophe, by the way, I forgot to tell you, she saw you change form in the alley the other night."

Christophe looked up at Lucius. "What do you mean?"

"Before your fight the other night, she was at the edge of the alley by the street and could see you change form before going on your rampage." Lucius looked up at him. "I figured you'd known that since you took the head off of her attacker as you exited the alley and tried to kill her after your transformation."

"I wasn't trying to kill her!" He looked at Jess with his eyes wide. "I wasn't trying to kill you, just trying to scare you off for your safety. I'm sorry you had to overhear everything. You need to leave now."

"No, not until you tell me if there is any chance of you changing your ways."

Christophe placed a hand on either of her shoulders and looked in her eyes. "I am beyond all hope. Leave now, I never want to see you again."

A tear fell from her eye as she turned and began walking out. Lucius called after her. "Stinks about Adam. He had such potential. Oh well, he'll fall easily enough."

Christophe looked at him. "Lucius, don't."

Jess turned. "Lucius. Not, Roman?" She nodded. "I knew there was something shady about you." She laughed. "I always like hearing about how you got your butt handed to you by Christ in the streets of New York."

Lucius nodded and grinned. "You think you'll be safe in New York? I can find you and dispatch you whenever and however I please. You'll be safe enough on the flight back. I won't give you the satisfaction of making your death that quick. Just keep your eyes open after your return. I'll keep you guessing for a while."

She took one last glance at Christophe and turned to leave. Lucius took a step in her direction and Christophe stepped between them and changed form. Jess heard roaring, bodies slamming against walls, and glass breaking as she stepped onto the elevator. Her tears were streaming.

# CHAPTER 29

Adam was sitting on the couch with the boys, when Jess walked in and gently shut the door. She faced the door and held onto the handle without turning around. Charlie and Justin looked from their mom to their dad.

"Why don't you boys go and start packing your bags."

They both got up simultaneously. Justin said, "Okay, daddy." They both walked towards their room, all the while, shooting worried glances toward Jessica. After the boys had shut their door, Adam stood and walked over to Jessica. He placed his hand on her arm and gently turned her towards him. As his eyes met her bloodshot eyes, she leaned her head into his chest as he wrapped her in a tight embrace. Her body went slack in his arms as she gave way to sobbing that caused her knees to give out. He lowered her to the floor. There they stayed, on their knees, by the door, with her losing all control, and him creating a self-contained bubble to allow her to vent without shame.

After her sobs subsided, she wrapped her arms around Adam's neck and kissed him. "Are you okay?"

She pulled back and wiped her eyes. She shook her head. "He's beyond help. He told me, flat out, that he would not change."

"I'm really sorry, hun." He pulled her into him, so her body leaned against his and her head rested on his shoulder. "Is there anything that I can do?"

She touched his arm. "Just this and listening."

# CHAPTER 30

As they packed their bags to head to the airport, a knock at the door echoed through the hotel suite. Adam and Jess looked at each other. Adam said, "I'll get it." Jess looked towards the door and then back to Adam and nodded. He stood up, placed his hand on the small of her back, and walked over to answer the door.

He opened the door to find Marco on the other side. His brow furrowed and his head and neck shrugged backwards. "Marco? What are you doing here?"

Jess came running out. "Marco?" She ran up and hugged him. "Please, come in." She looked at Adam. "Is that any way to treat a guest?"

Marco pinched the back of Adam's arm. "Yeah. Is that any way to treat a guest? Silly boy."

Adam winced and rubbed the back of his arm. "My deepest apologies." He lowered his arm.

Jess asked, "How did you find us?"

Adam smirked. "Yeah, Marco! How did you find us?"

Marco turned, "I have contacts at the hotel who let me know you were here. After the attack and all of you disappearing afterward, I grew worried."

Marco smirked at Adam as Adam thought. *Show off. I'll get one over on you one of these days.*

"Has my father been back to the apartment?"

Marco's eyes lowered. "No, sweetie. He hasn't." Jess nodded. "You know him, dear. He's probably just staying at his office."

Adam piped up. "Is there a reason you're here? They do have a plane to catch."

Marco reached up and grabbed Adam by the ear. He pulled to where Adam was bent at the waist, wincing and whimpering in pain. "Rudeness, again?" He pulled harder on Adam's lobe, twisted it, and then let go. "We'll get you trained soon enough."

Adam stood back up and was rubbing his ear. "Fair enough."

Marco laughed while looking at Adam. His expression went from jovial to caring as he looked from Adam to Jess. "Actually, I've come to escort all of you to the airport."

Jess' brow furrowed and her voice quieted. "How did you know that we were heading to the airport?"

Marco smiled. "As I said before, and the genius here just said, I have connections." He looked at Adam. "In some ways, I've always thought of myself as your guardian angel."

Adam rolled his eyes, shook his head, and headed for the bedroom to finish packing. "You all catch up; I'll finish packing."

Jess asked after him, "Are you sure?"

Adam looked back right before he disappeared through the door. "No problem at all."

As he finished packing Jessica's bag, he could hardly hear the two talking. Although, what they were discussing was not what concerned him. The reason behind Michael escorting him to the airport was the question lingering in his mind.

A few minutes later, he heard Justin say from their room, "We've got our bags packed, mommy." A second later, he heard footsteps running out into the main area of the suite and the boys saying in unison, "Marco!"

Charlie then asked, "What are you doing here?"

Marco said in a voice pointed towards Adam's location. "You are so much like your father. I'm actually here to go with you to the airport."

Justin asked, "Are you going back to New York with us?"

Jess laughed. "No, dear one. I'm only going with you to the airport. I prefer Chicago style pizza over New York style."

Charlie responded, "So do I, but don't tell my daddy. He likes New York style."

Marco and Jess laughed. "That's perfectly fine, buddy. There's nothing wrong with that. You love him just the same, don't you?"

"Mmhmm."

Adam laughed under his breath. "You're hilarious, Marco. Just wait, I'll get you one way or another."

Marco's voice said from the doorway. "Adam, don't you know it isn't healthy to talk to yourself? People, … may think you're crazy."

Adam smiled. "It's not talking to yourself that makes you crazy, only when you start asking yourself questions and then answering those questions. You wouldn't know about that would you, Marco?" Marco opened his mouth to speak. Adam placed his hand on Marco's arm. "Wait." He tilted his head as if listening to something in the other room. "I think I hear Ozzy playing your theme song."

Marco tilted his ear towards the ceiling. "I think I hear Karen Carpenter singing yours. Well, at least the song that makes me think of you."

Adam grinned. "Which song might that be, Top of the World or Superstar?"

Marco shook his head. "Neither, Rainy Days and Mondays." Adam's expression flattened. Marco looked down and then back up. He then spoke in a whisper. "Actually, I came in to tell you that Simon will meet with Jess and the kids once they get back to New York."

He paused and stared at Jess' suitcase lying on the bed. "Simon. Simon. Why does that name sound familiar?"

"He's the man that put Jude in the hospital and caused him to receive his gift."

"He put Jude in the hospital, and you want me to trust him with my family?"

Marco stepped closer to Adam. "Adam, think of who this is coming from. You know that we would not put Jess and the boys in harm's way. Simon and Jude had another run in together that left Simon changed. He is helping those in need and if he were to stray, Jude would know it."

Adam nodded. "Fair enough. At least they'll be safe." He paused, looked, and listened towards Jess and the kids' location. "Are you two any closer to figuring out the monster's identity?"

Michael started fidgeting with one of the latches on Jess's luggage. He shook his head. "No. Have you?"

Adam shook his head. "No. With Jess and the boys back

in New York, we'll be able to focus more on figuring out who we're up against and how they tie in to all these murders."

# CHAPTER 31

**B**arry Piper grabbed the last of the bags to carry into the cabin. With deadlines fast approaching, he had spent little time with his family over the previous months. After a discussion with his wife, Elizabeth, they decided that a family camping trip would be the perfect getaway from the chaos of work and the city.

He heard the voices of their oldest children, Mary and Robert. As he closed the hatch of their SUV, he saw them standing on the porch. Mary looked at him. "Dad, can Robert and I walk down to the lake?"

Barry looked towards the water 300 feet away from the cabin. The shore could easily be seen from where he stood, or anywhere close for that matter. "Sure." The kids ran off the porch and towards the water. Barry yelled after them, "Don't get too close to the water!" Mary raised her arm and waved in response. He watched them for a few seconds longer, smiled, and climbed the steps towards the cabin's front door.

Elizabeth was handing Anthony, their youngest, a cookie as he walked through the door. She glanced towards the window. "I think we made a good decision. They seem to be enjoying themselves already."

Barry looked out of the window as he walked towards her. "It would seem so."

"Did you have anything extra planned for the weekend, or was coming here about the end of your thought process?"

He leaned on the island across from her. "That was the main thought, but I'm sure I can think of a few things we can do while we're up here." He winked. Barry stood and walked around the island and wrapped Elizabeth in his arms. "Of course, some of what I have in mind will have to wait until the kids are in bed."

She touched her lips to his. "Is that so?"

"Mmhmm."

"In that case, maybe we ought to make it an early night."

He kissed her once more and released the embrace. He walked back around to where he had placed the bags. As he picked one up, he said, "Well, I suppose I had better get everything unpacked sooner than later."

She bit her lip while undressing him with her eyes. "That would be a good idea."

Elizabeth watched him as he climbed the stairs and entered the master bedroom.

Shadows engulfed the room as the three tall windows behind her exploded. Two masses flew past her wearing familiar clothing. The last thing she saw were two vertical rows of massive teeth closing together in front of her face.

Barry rushed from the room out onto the landing. His

eyes came to rest on a large creature with its mouth resting on top of his wife's neck, where her head had been, just moments before. Her body slumped to the floor. Anthony sat on the floor screaming. Barry stepped towards the stairs. As he did, the creature pivoted its head to where a single eye glared up at him.

It stomped a taloned foot down onto Anthony and ground it back and forth, silencing the deafening screams. A tear rolled down Barry's cheek. The beast jumped from the kitchen onto the outside of the railing opposite him. The monster's claws penetrated the fleshy part of Barry's lower jaw and exited through the top of his head.

It lifted him off his feet and over the railing. The creature held him in mid-air watching his wide eyes as his body twitched. After the movements stopped, the monster swung its arm in a wide arc and flung him, like a spiked football, to the floor below.

# CHAPTER 32

As they walked from the drop off area to print their tickets, Adam and Jess walked hand in hand. Her suitcase in his opposite hand. Marco, trailed close behind carrying a twin in each arm. Adam studied the people as they walked. He watched for anyone that seemed out of place. As they stood to the side as Jess acquired their tickets and gate number, Adam glanced around. He noticed how a lot of older women were looking at Marco with bedroom eyes.

"Marco, when all this is done, you can feel free to take the boys out if it will help you get a date with an older woman."

Adam's face had pulled into a tight smirk when Marco looked at him. Marco's mouth stretched into a huge smile. "I may just have to accept that offer."

Adam's expression dropped. "What?"

"To you they may be old, but to me," He looked at one of

the women and dipped his head. "they're new and as refreshing as a spring rain."

Jess walked up smiling. "What are you two talking about that has you smirking and smiling?"

Both directed their eyes away. Adam and Marco said in unison, "Nothing."

Charles spoke up. "They were talking about Marco using Justin and I to get dates with old women."

Jess shot Adam a stern, sarcastic glare. "Oh, were they now?"

"Uh huh. Marco said they're new and refreshing as a spring rain."

She grinned and looked at Marco. "You definitely think young, don't you, Marco?"

"That I do, Miss Jessica."

She placed her palm on Marco's cheek. "If you take the boys to help you pick up women, you'd better treat them to dinner."

"Of course, I'd treat the women to dinner."

"The boys."

Marco stood agape for a second. "Oh, of course, Miss Jessica. That would be only natural. I would spoil these boys rotten, given the chance."

She lowered her hand and nodded. "Maybe, once it's safer to come back to The Windy City, we can set something up."

She looked at Adam, grinned, and pushed up his chin closing his open mouth. "What? You thought that I wouldn't be cool with it?"

"Actually, I figured you'd be totally against the idea."

"Heck no. Marco's like an adopted uncle, who I would be more than happy to help in finding love or, at least, some pleasant company."

As Jess placed her hand back in Adam's he grinned. "Well said, Sweetheart. We will definitely get something going, once all this mess is resolved."

For the rest of the walk to the security check point, no one said a word. As they stopped at the edge of the entry point, Adam looked at Jess. "Simon, will meet you when you land. He'll either be holding a sign or you'll know him when you see him. Jude says he has noticeable scars on his face."

Jess nodded and kissed Adam. As she pulled away, she said, "I love you."

"I love you, too."

"I'll call you when we land."

Adam nodded. "Sounds good."

Marco handed him each of the twins in turn. He hugged and kissed both boys and put them down. "You all have a safe trip."

Jess nodded and a tear rolled down her cheek. "We will. You be careful and watch each other's backs."

Marco and Adam said, "We will."

Jess shot Marco a curious look. He grinned and shrugged. "You know how dangerous Chicago can be."

She nodded. "Keep safe, Marco. There's a lot more going on here than simple gang wars and street violence."

"Will do, Miss Jessica." She nodded, looked at Adam, mouthed, "I love you", and turned to enter the queue.

The two turned to walk back to the car. Adam watched people coming and going. "So, genius." He glanced at Marco. "What's the game plan?"

"The plan," He placed his hand on Adam's shoulder. "is to meet up back at the hotel and then get something eat. I'm starving. Then, we can discuss options over dinner."

# CHAPTER 33

J ude was sitting at the table holding a steaming cup of coffee as they walked in. He looked from his cup to Adam. "It took you long enough."

Adam looked at him as they approached the table and sat down in two of the other chairs. "Were you that excited to see us? Although, Chicago traffic isn't as bad as New York's, it's still traffic none the less."

Jude grinned and sipped from his cup. "Did Jess and the boys make it off alright?"

Adam nodded. "Yeah, they did. Michael told me that one of your acquaintances will be meeting them."

Jude looked at Michael. "Simon?" Michael nodded and Jude looked back at Adam. "They're in good hands. They will be safe with him." Adam nodded his acceptance.

Michael spoke up. "As far as more pressing matters go,

have either of you been able to dig up anything on who we are up against?"

Adam looked at Michael with a glint of sarcasm. "You mean other than Lucius?"

Michael looked at Adam. "Duh." Michael smirked, then his expression flattened. "I know we've briefly discussed it before, but… are you sure that he never told you any of his future plans?"

Adam shook his head. "He never said a word regarding his future plans." He tapped his knuckles on the table. "Ever since joining the two of you, I have been running everything through my head: words, actions, …and even body language. There was no hint of future plans." He looked to Jude and back to Michael. "It's like he was always living in the moment."

Jude took a sip of coffee and set down his cup. "What do we know of the victims?"

Michael and Adam looked at Jude. Michael said, "A couple politicians, a few underground kingpins, a businessman, and his family."

Jude asked, "How are they connected?"

Michael drummed his fingers on the table. "That's the question we need answered. The identity of the beast should answer that question."

The three remained quiet contemplating possibilities for a few seconds when Michael burst out, full of energy, "So, who's hungry?"

* * *

As the three sat around the table, since he had not fully informed Adam and Jude of the details of the upcoming days,

Michael figured that he would give the two a decent meal before the grueling days to come.

Michael sipped from his glass of water, set it on the table, and looked from one to the other. "With the chaotic events of the last few days, I haven't had a chance to speak much to either of you about the training and what it will consist of over the coming days. Do either of you have any questions?"

He looked at Jude and Adam in turn and both looked at the table in contemplation. Jude's brow rose. "How intense will this training be?"

Michael took another sip of water. "This will be the most difficult thing that either of you have faced so far."

Adam spoke up. "The monster?"

Jude shot Adam a curious look with one eyebrow raised. Michael answered. "No, Adam. This training will be the most difficult experience of your life."

Adam looked up to Michael and, seeing a level gaze, looked back down at the black tablecloth beneath his hands. "Oh."

"The training will not kill you." He looked towards the ceiling with a thoughtful stare. "Although, some of our previous trainees have wished for death while going through it."

Adam looked up to Jude. "Are you sure," He pointed to Michael with his thumb. "...he's not the one that we're up against and not Lucius?"

Jude smirked. Michael put his hand out towards Adam. "Shh. We don't know if Lucius has anyone within earshot."

"Do you sense him close by?"

"No, but that doesn't mean he doesn't have allies in this room listening in. Besides, he is pretty much everywhere."

Adam's brow furrowed. "Minions?"

Michael let out a sign. "Yes and no."

Jude looked at Michael, dumbfounded. "How is it both?"

Michael turned towards Jude. "A lot of Christians seem to believe that only God is omnipresent. Yet, they always seem to claim that Satan is always watching and waiting, which indicates that he is ever-present."

Adam asked, "What about hallowed ground?"

Michael turned to Adam. "'Let he who is without sin…'" Adam nodded. "The ground may be consecrated, but humans are still human and imperfect. As long as anything is present within the human mind: sin, fear, guilt, doubts…he is present within those thoughts and minds."

Jude looked up as the waiter approached with a tray. "Seems like a logical argument."

Michael said as the man approached with their orders. "No argument about it, I've had to address that point for centuries."

The waiter paused and raised his brow. Jude spoke up. "Discussing character description for a role-playing game."

The man nodded. "I had a phase like that once. Of course, I was much younger, but you three definitely look the part."

Adam looked at his cohorts. Seeing them both in grungy t-shirts and hair tussled, he laughed. "We do look the part. Don't we?"

As the waiter walked away, Michael said, "On second thought, I'll just wait until your training starts to discuss the details with you. Be sure to eat your fill. You're going to need it."

# CHAPTER 34

After the bill was paid, the three exited the restaurant. Adam and Jude hunched their shoulders and crossed their arms. As their brows furrowed, their breath escaped in white whisps. All of them looked up and down the street and sidewalks at people coming and going.

Adam said in a louder voice than expected. "So, where are we headed to train?"

Jude kept his eyes forward. "Adam, I don't think they heard you. Would you like a bullhorn?"

"You don't think *who* heard me?"

"The entire city." Jude turned to face Adam. "Keep your voice down. Will you?"

Adam nodded. Michael said while grinning, "You'll know soon enough. Hopefully, your bodies will be okay, while we're gone."

Adam turned, wide eyed, towards Michael. "Our bodies?"

"Yeah. Some of our older allies had their bodies eaten by rats and other animals while they were away for training." He smirked. "Should have seen their expressions when we had to tell them that they had no physical form to return to."

Michael turned and started walking away from the restaurant. Adam and Jude jumped and followed on his heels. Adam croaked after him. "You're serious, aren't you?"

Continuing to walk forward, Michael looked back over his shoulder as Adam had just caught up. "Yes. I'm completely serious." He turned down the next alleyway. "Which is why we stopped that practice after the first few times."

"Why not after the first time?"

"We tried Guardians the second time. Lucius attacked my soldiers in my absence and mutilated the bodies of the trainees."

Adam glanced down at the dark ground as they came to a stop. He saw wrappers and grime coating the pavement at his feet. Michael stood with his back towards the wall. "I'm sorry to hear that."

Michael nodded. "Thank you. I'm sorry that I have to say it. They were fantastic angels and even better warriors."

"Is there such a thing as a bad angel?"

Jude furrowed his brow while looking at Adam. "Really?"

Adam looked up at Jude. "What? It's a valid quest…" Jude pinched the bridge of his nose as Adam's face went slack as his shame set in. "Point taken."

Michael cocooned himself and the others within his wings. He grew quiet as his wing feathers lifted with rising air. Jude and Adam glanced around and then to Michael.

Michael's eyelids flew open to reveal glowing, pearlescent eyes. The light fluctuated within the orbs giving them the look of illuminated marble.

"You two may want to keep your eyes closed."

Adam croaked, "Will it be that bright?"

The illuminated eyes settled on him. "No. You just don't want to see what this will do to your bodies."

Adam started fidgeting. "I want out!"

Michael shook his head. "It's too late, you're in this for the long run. Brace yourselves because this is going to be excruciating."

Adam screamed and motioned to escape when the space within Michael's wings filled with a blinding white light and the three disappeared from the alley.

# CHAPTER 35

They rubbed their eyes and eased them open as Michael folded his wings behind his back. Adam glanced down at his body and frantically patted his chest and face. His expression relaxed with an exhaled sigh. "I thought you said it was going to hurt?" He looked at Jude. "I didn't feel a thing. Did you?"

Jude placed his hands on either side of Adam's face. "You should know by now to have a little more faith in Michael and not to be so gullible." He smacked the side of Adams face three times and stepped away.

A booming laugh rang out from a few feet away. "Michael, are these the heroes we're meant to train? These can't be them. The one seems too simple minded and the other seems no more than bone."

Michael looked up and grinned. "Hello, Gabriel. Believe

it or not, there's more to these two than meets the eye."

Gabriel looked from Adam to Jude, measuring them up in turn. "We shall see." He waved them his direction. "Come, there is much to do to prepare you for what's ahead." As they passed him, he glanced at them again. "Hopefully, not as much preparation as what I expect you'll need."

Michael stepped towards Gabriel and offered his arm. Gabriel accepted, clasping Michael's forearm in his hand. "It's good to see you, brother."

"You as well." They released each other's arms and turned to walk towards the training area. "You should visit home more often."

As they began walking, they realized Adam and Jude had stopped and began staring at the massive white void. Their bodies cast no shadow. Gabriel and Michael elbowed their way through the two. As they moved through, Michael slapped Jude on his shoulder. "Look familiar?"

Jude shook his head. "Not at all."

"This is where we first spoke after your skirmish in the alley."

"I thought that had been a dream or a figment of my imagination."

Michael shook his head and Gabriel laughed and said to Michael, "The same response once again."

Michael grinned towards Gabriel and gave a single nod. He returned his eyes to Jude. "Every bit of it was real."

Jude gave a slow nod. "So, I have been to the training grounds before."

"Yes and no." Jude's brow rose. "This is more of an 'as needed' area. It changes to whatever we need it to be at the time."

Jude looked around in awe. "Was I dead when I was here

before?"

Michael's voice was high and strained. "Technically..."

Jude's eyes snapped to Michael. "You waited until now to tell me?" Michael pursed his lips and then gave a quick nod. "Why not tell me then?" Michael shrugged his shoulders with a tilt of his head. Gabriel began scratching the back of his head and looking around. "Am I dead or can I count myself among the living?"

Michael raised his hand with index figure extended. "Wait... I know this one." Jude's mouth flattened. "The living."

"You're sure?"

Michael looked to Gabriel and smiled. "Absolutely." Looking back at Jude with an educated haughtiness. "The last time you were here, it was more of an out of body experience than being dead." Jude's brow furrowed. "If you had been dead, I would have given you a choice if you wanted to stay or go on living a regular life."

"So, I wasn't dead or at risk of dying."

Michael smiled. "I wouldn't go as far as to say that."

Jude shook his head. "You're maddening."

Gabriel and Michael roared with laughter. Gabriel slapped Michael on the shoulder. "Is he always this serious?"

"For the most part, but he does have his moments." Michael looked to Jude through wet eyes. "Jude, you should really take your own advice. Don't take everything I say so serious." Jude's eyes dropped, along with his pride. They raised back to meet Michael's. "You were close to death, but you were safe in our hands."

Jude nodded. "So, when do we start?"

As Michael spread his wings. The void changed into, what looked like, Chicago. Angels began plummeting from rooftops with wings extended. "Right now."

Jude and Adam transformed as they started moving forward. After they walked past, Gabriel looked at Adam. "Things have certainly changed over the years. I remember when we used to give them stronger armor and weaponry."

Michael placed his hand on Gabriel's shoulder. "If you think about it, it really hasn't."

# CHAPTER 36

As the plane touched down at JFK, Jessica began grabbing the carry-ons. She looked at the boys. "Are you two ready?"

Charlie took his bag from her. "Yep."

Jess smiled. "Thank you two, for being so good."

Justin took his bag and gave her a one-armed hug. "You're welcome, mommy."

The entire flight, Jess had been watching the other passengers to see if she was being watched. She grew even more alert as they departed the plane. To her relief, everyone seemed like they were going about their lives as normal. As they exited the security area, Jess wondered if she would know who she was supposed to be meeting. She did not want to stand there staring at all the people standing around or ask every person in the area if they were the person that she was supposed to be meeting. As she approached the group of onlookers, she noticed a man with a large scar across his face. It was clear that it had been left by a large animal. At noticing her gaze as she neared, she could see recognition in his eyes. "Simon?"

He smiled. "Hi, you must be Jessica."

"Yes, I am." She reached out to shake his hand. As he accepted, Charlie stepped towards him.

Simon looked down at him. "What's up, little man?"

Charlie grabbed Simon's coat sleeve and tugged down on it twice. Simon bent down closer to Charlie. As Charlie reached up and touched the scar, he asked, "What happened to your face?"

Jess grabbed the collar of Charlie's jacket and pulled him back towards her. "Charlie, you apologize this instant. That was very rude."

Charlie's brow furrowed. He looked up at Simon, almost on the verge of tears. "I'm sorry, Mr. Simon."

Simon knelt down to eye level with him. "That's okay, bud. This was given to me from a friend."

Charlie's brow rose. "Why would a friend do that to you?"

"Well, you see, Charlie, I wasn't always a good person. So, my friend gave me these scars to always remind me that I should try to be a better person."

"Are you?"

"I would like to think I am. The only thing I can do is my best." Simon stood and met Jessica's eye. "Tell you what...my afternoon is completely free, how does lunch sound?" Her brow furrowed. "From what I was told, you've had a lot going on the last few days."

"That would be putting it mildly."

Simon nodded. "My treat."

Jessica smiled. "If you insist."

They turned and began walking towards the parking gar-age.

# Chapter 37

Christophe walked along Wilson Avenue. It was just after nightfall and darkness had settled over the city. His mind wandered deeper with each step.

He wondered how much power he could eventually possess. A memory flashed in his mind of a young Jessica swinging on her playset in their backyard. A corner of his mouth curled upward. She used to spend hours swinging back and forth.

Another few steps… *you wanted me to allow you to discover yourself as you grew. I wish you could respect me doing the same now. I know that I've focused on my success, even above you and your mother.*

He walked further, passing people as he went. His clothing was casual: a hoodie, jeans, and tennis shoes. Attire that would have not attracted too much attention. Christophe smiled knowing that anyone who would try and give him trouble, would be way out of their league.

He was nearing the Lake Shore Drive viaduct. His nostrils flared with the scent of the destitute that frequented it for shelter. Christophe's eyes flitted between shadows moving under the streetlights entering and exiting the underpass of the road he walked along.

Homeless people, how he despised them. They rarely tried to better themselves or get back onto their feet. It was always he and his wealthy business associates that had to pick up the slack to fund programs that they never took advantage of.

*May as well free myself of some of the burden. Granted, it will be a drop in the bucket, but it will at least scare more of the population away from the main city streets.*

Christophe took stock of his immediate surroundings. There was a short, middle-aged man about 20 feet ahead of him. As the man approached, he saw a set of headlights cresting the road above the overpass. Further to his right, the pavement and landscape began to illuminate and brighten from the opposite direction.

The man glanced at him and quickly lowered his gaze. Christophe took two steps to close the gap between himself and the pedestrian. As he did, his feet grew in size and shape. His perspective changed as well. When his clawed hand engulfed the man's head and torso, Christophe's eyes were peering down on him from 20 feet in the air.

In an overhand arc, he launched the wriggling body through the windshield of the oncoming car. There was no sound of screeching tires, only the shattering of glass. He turned in time to intercept the sedan approaching from his rear. A massive, clawed hand sank into the hood and grasped the bumper and the front cross section of the car's chassis. He lifted the car off the ground and turned in time to stop the other car with the obliterated windshield a few feet away. With his free hand, he picked it up the same way as the sedan.

He walked closer to the overpass and launched the sedan over Lakeshore Drive to block the far viaduct entrance on the left side of the bridge. After a few seconds had passed, enough for confusion to set in amongst those inhabiting the tunnel, he launched the other vehicle to block the closer entrance on his left. He grinned as the roof of the car crushed, at least two, people as it slammed to the ground.

Christophe lowered his body and extended his frills. He grinned as he saw the pavement glow orange. He launched off the street over the far edge of the overpass. His body pivoted in mid-air, and he landed on Lakeshore Drive, facing into the viaduct. Half of the occupants were still focused on the vehicles, the others turned at the rumble through the pavement as he landed. They had started screaming as he unleashed a torrent of molten material throughout the tunnel, turning it into a giant oven. After a few seconds, cracking and groaning could be heard as the supports gave way and the Wilson overpass collapsed onto Lakeshore Drive.

# CHAPTER 38

G abriel and Michael flew in heightened circles study-
ing the fray. They watched Jude and Adam's movements and actions, for strengths and weaknesses.

After a few more moments of examining their subjects,
Gabriel and Michael dove down to make an attack on the duo.
Michael drew his sword as he drew closer to Jude. At seeing
movement and smelling Michael coming nearer, Jude glanced
up and started into a backflip. Jude saw a flash of silver inches
from his eyes at the arc of his movement.

Michael failed to notice that he was being closely watched
by Adam. As he followed through with his attack on Jude, he
made it a few feet before a serpentine jaw clamped around his
torso.

Jude landed and crouched on his feet. He turned and
grinned at seeing Michael clinched in Adam's jaw. He saw

Gabriel flying in for an attack from behind Adam. Jude took off in a sprint. Adam lowered his head as Jude jumped and placed his feet at the center of Adam's head. The snake catapulted Jude through the air towards Gabriel. Gabriel's eyes widened.

Gabriel attempted to bank right, a millisecond too late. Jude grabbed Gabriel's left wing near his back and pulled himself closer to him. When in reach, he latched onto the right wing just like the left. He leaned in close to Gabriel's ear. "Nice try, Gabriel. I hope you're ready for a ride." Jude leaned back and forced both wings closed. The two plummeted 30 feet towards the ground. They were a few feet from crashing when Jude jumped from Gabriel's back, tucked into a roll, and sprang up onto his feet. He turned to face Gabriel.

Gabriel lay for a couple seconds without moving. He pushed himself up and sat back with his legs underneath him. His face was plastered with a wide grin. Jude walked over to him and offered his hand. Gabriel accepted and Jude helped him to his feet.

"You pack a few more surprises than I gave you credit for."

Jude laughed. "We do tend to keep a few tricks up our sleeves, just in case."

Gabriel pursed his lips and nodded. "Smart idea. It looks like there is, at least, one thing we won't have to teach you."

"Always have a backup plan."

Michael and Adam approached the two. Adam looked at Jude. "Nice distance." He looked at Gabriel. "You alright? You face planted pretty hard."

"Yeah, I'm grand." He looked at Michael. "You doing, okay? No puncture wounds?"

Michael laughed. "Nope, I'm still intact and not leaking

anywhere." He looked back and forth between Jude and Adam. "Are you two ready for a break?"

They looked at each other and nodded. Jude responded, "Yeah, I would say we could use a rest."

Michael nodded. "In that case, let's take a walk. I have something to show the both of you."

They walked through what still looked like inner-city Chicago. After walking for about a mile, Michael turned and entered what looked like a warehouse. Adam and Jude exchanged glances, shrugged, and followed him.

They stepped through the door and their eyes adjusted in an instant. In the rear corner of the building, they saw lines of forges with anvils in front of them. To their left, stood rows of racks holding countless weapons glinting in the light filtering in from outside. Workbenches lined the front right corner of the facility. Etching tools and hammers hung from organizers on the benches. The lighting shone brighter from the back right corner. They could see shining objects in the more abundant lighting. The pieces were displayed in elegance even though its only purpose was for storage. It was displayed as if it were part of a museum showcase.

It was to this last section in which Michael was heading. The two followed him without questioning his motives.

Both looked around in amazement. The farther they walked, the longer the building seemed to stretch. As they made it closer to the armor storage, Jude said, "I thought all of this was a figment of our imagination."

"You should have already figured out that wasn't exactly the case." Jude's brow furrowed. "You've been interacting with your surroundings this entire time. The building and the majority of its contents are physical manifestations of what I have imagined."

"So, if one of us were to take something from here that is a physical representation of something concocted in your mind, it would disappear upon our return to the moral world?"

Michael turned and walked backwards while facing Jude. "There it is."

Jude glanced over his shoulder. "There what is?"

Michael sneered. "The proof that you're smarter than you look." Michael winked at him. "The only objects in this building that would travel to the mortal world would be ones that actually exist."

Jude nodded. "Nice security measure."

Adam looked from Jude to Michael. "What security measure?"

Michael raised a brow. "I honestly thought you were better at piecing things together, Adam." He looked at Jude. "Would you mind explaining it to him?"

"Not a problem. If all of this were real, it would be a major risk." Adam's brow furrowed and his forked tongue flicked out of his mouth. "If Lucius happened to read our thoughts, he would find out what kind of arms they were stockpiling against him. This way, it would be impossible to find out the size of the actual weapons and armor cache."

"Oh, why didn't I come to that conclusion?"

Michael looked at him. "I was wondering the same thing. Is the stress of the situation messing with your thoughts?"

"Not that I can tell, but then again, it is sometimes difficult for a person to tell when they're not functioning at full mental clarity. This situation has had me mentally pulled in numerous directions, maybe my focus or clarity is slipping a bit."

Michael nodded. "We've all noticed it. At first, I thought it was just a moronic moment, but as the occurrences grew more progressive, I began wondering if there was a reasonable underlying cause."

"I'm sorry." He lowered his head. "I can try to do better."

Michael stopped and walked towards Adam. He drew his sword. At the sound of unsheathing metal, Adam tucked his head even lower. Michael placed the pommel of his sword into the hollow behind the point of Adam's lower jaw and used it to lift Adam's head. "Look at me." Michael could see embarrassment and fear in the red and gold marbled orbs. "When I want an apology from you...you'll know it. There is nothing you need apologize for, given the current situation." The eyes looked away.

Michael rotated the sword. "Stay focused. Your family was attacked by the monster we're trying to identify and defeat. You went out of a window willing to sacrifice yourself for their safety. You have no reason to be ashamed. You have been a valiant fighter, father, and husband. You continue standing proud and with honor." Michael looked around. "You are not alone. We are right here with you and promise to look after Jess and the boys as if they were our own. I can't speak for Jude, but I know that all of heaven loves them as much as you do. Stand firm and have faith. We will not abandon you."

Adam closed his eyes. When he opened them, they were clear and at peace. Michael placed his palm gently on the crown of Adam's head behind his eyes. He turned and sheathed his sword as he approached the armor displayed before them.

As Michael approached the armor, Jude stepped over to Adam. He watched the marbled eye look up at him. Jude placed his hand behind Adam's eye on his head. He turned and began walking towards Michael.

Jude stepped up next to the angel. He admired the piece in front of them. "We finally made it."

"Yeah, I figured you two could use an extra cool down with the intensity of your training efforts."

"Thank you for that. An extra stretch and breather are definitely appreciated." He lifted his chin towards the suit of armor in front of them. "Nice set. Is it one of the fake ones?"

Michael stepped closer to the armor that he had admired once before. "No, this is one of the real pieces. The last time that I laid eyes on this was during one of my last conversations with Christ." He ran his hands over the armor to examine it for imperfections. Michael looked from the glistening armor to Jude. Jude's eyes were wide and his mouth agape. "Do you like it?"

"It's stunning. Other than decrease the amount of damage taken, can it do anything else?"

Michael walked back towards Jude. "That all depends on you."

"What do you mean?"

"It's yours. We shall know soon enough what a few of those possibilities are when you learn the feel of the armor." He motioned for a few of the nearby angels to approach. As they neared, he said to them, "Get Jude into his armor."

"Right away, Sir."

Michael turned to Adam. "Follow me and I'll take you to yours." He placed his hand on Jude's shoulder and walked away.

Adam followed, close behind him, scanning the area for a long suit of armor that would fit a serpent body of his size. Michael stopped and turned to face Adam. At still not seeing any armor that was made for him, he looked at Michael. "You did have armor made for me as well. Didn't you?"

Michael chuckled. "Bring it down."

Adam looked up to see a gigantic suit of armor that looked as if it were made of solid silver. As it lowered, he got a closer look and found that, other than the head covering, it consisted of body encompassing sections joined by single lengths in between that would hug his spine. He grew curious as to how he would be able to move but had this answered as he studied the basic nature of the armor as it was lowered. The thin sections he thought were between the larger pieces actually ran the entire length of the piece and was fluid. When it had lowered to eye level, he could see intricate designs etched into the entire length of the armor. The helmet of the piece covered the majority of his head to just behind his nostrils. It had two daggers jutting out and running parallel to the helmet. It also had two lower shrouds that angled down behind his eyes and ran along his lower jaw.

Michael watched his reaction with a wide smile. "Is this what you were expecting?"

Adam's turquoise head shook. "No. This is so much more than what I imagined. It's amazing."

"You have no idea." He looked at the angels who had just lowered the armor. "Help him into this."

"Yes, Sir."

Michael looked at Adam. "Once you and Jude are in your armor, meet Gabriel and I by the entrance. I need to speak with him about a few things before we get started again."

Adam nodded and turned his attention towards the angels and his armor.

# Chapter 39

Christophe stepped off the elevator to the scent of charred wood. He glanced left and then looked right. Walking over to the once broken window, he ran his hand along it to admire the quality of the repair. His eyes glazed over as he stared at the street below. After a few moments had passed, he turned and headed towards his charred penthouse entrance. He placed his hand along the blackened door frame as he stepped through. Looking around as he entered, he called out to Jess, knowing that only silence would respond.

His steps echoed throughout the penthouse as he checked each room, imaging his family walking through the apartment and activities or conversations that might have taken place. Nothing was left in their rooms. He inhaled trying to catch lingering whiffs of their scents. His nose picked up that

Jessica's scent was stronger than the others. Turning his head towards the living room, he noticed that her scent grew stronger in that direction. He turned and began tracking the source. It led him past the living room and to his bedroom. Standing in his bedroom doorway, he glanced around to find an envelope lying on his nightstand. He exhaled through his nose, walked over, and picked up the envelope as he sat down on his bed.

Upon opening it, he saw Jessica's cursive handwriting in black ink.

*Dad,*

*I have decided, for my family's safety, to leave. I know your secret. I think you knew that I was in the alley the other night. You're attack on us had me curious as to the motive behind the attack, until I witnessed your transformation in the alley. I keep holding out hope that you can turn to good, but also wonder, with how dedicated you were to your career while I was growing up, if you attacked us to prove to yourself that we are less important than your success.*

*When you saved me that night, it gave me hope that you could change. If it was just my safety at risk, based on my hopes, I would gladly stick around a while longer. Unfortunately, the other nights attack being directed towards the twins that makes my staying a moot point.*

*All I can do is hope and pray that you have a change of heart. I wish our family would have gotten more consideration and love over the years. It's a shame. We were worth it.*

*In the slim chance a miracle happens, and you do have a change of heart, you know my number.*

*Love Always,*
*Jess*

Christophe sat and stared at the letter in his hands. He began talking to the empty room. "She has every right to give up hope. I have been a horrible father."

A voice that sounded similar to a cross between a crow and a reptile responded from the silence. *"You have been a provider. You've always made sure she had what she needed and wanted."*

He set the letter on the nightstand and stood up to seek out the source of the voice. "Who are you and what do you want?"

*"I want your complete devotion and loyalty."*

Christophe went to the doorway and looked out into the living room. "Where are you?"

The voice responded with a hissing caw, *"Go to the window."*

As he stepped up to the glass, he looked on the city below. "How can you be…"

Something in his peripheral vision seemed off. At first it appeared like a dark green blur. He focused on what he thought was a smudge on the window pane. Two glowing eyes flickered to light. A reptilian reflection stared back at him. *"I am you."*

"You're not me."

*"I am your other self; The one you've always aspired to be. The part of you that has always sacrificed for wealth and power…that's me. You are stronger, more powerful, and more intimidating."*

Christophe glanced down at the letter. "We know what you've cost me." He looked back at his reflection. "My question now is…what can you give me?"

Sharp teeth were shadowed from a throaty glow as the reflection grinned. *"Everything."* The voice purred in pleasure.

The face faded back into his human reflection. He stood staring into the eyes staring back at him. His gaze passed through his reflection and distanced beyond the horizon.

"Why can't everything be as simple as black and white? It's always that gray area that causes confusion and frustration. I've always loved my family and have been pushing myself for success in my career. I thought that I had been successful at keeping the balance between the two. Apparently, I was mistaken. She's wanting my devotion aligned with my family and not my career. Kings and Queens of old had family and power. Why shouldn't I have both? I sold my soul for money and power."

He picked up the letter. "In truth, did I ever want a family more than my career and success." He looked back at his reflection. "Did you, or was the family just more of a luxury than a necessity?" He cycled through memories searching for the truth. In every memory he could recall thinking about business meetings and brainstorming plans, mergers, and market values. The time he spent with family was always overshadowed by work and climbing the corporate ladder. He looked down at Jessica's handwritten pages. "Sorry, baby girl, some bridges are better left burnt." His fingertips began to glow, and her letter burst into flames. He stood and watched until only embers remained in his hand.

He looked down upon the city. "Let's get this city shaken up more than we already have." He turned and walked back into the living room to leave the penthouse. A familiar scent stopped him in place. He inhaled deep and he tried retracing where he was when he smelled the scent before. His eyes opened as he exhaled and fell upon the blackened entryway and his brow furrowed.

The large blue snake flashed through is memory. "Of course, he had smelled him all along."

He breathed in again, separating the scents within the room. Christophe began listing the smells as his mind recognized their familiarity. "Jessica, Justin, Charlie..." His eyes went wide. "Why didn't I recognize that scent on him sooner? I wonder if he's figured out my identity yet. If Jess told him, then he may already know." He began moving again to head down to street level. "No matter. It looks like I'll just have to give my son-in-law a little extra attention."

# CHAPTER 40

G abriel and Michael stood on a nearby rooftop and studied how well Adam and Jude were adjusting to their new armor. They were amazed at how quickly they were adapting to it.

Jude's armor had gone through one transformation early on. When flexed in the right manor, the tips of the glove fingers extended to a six-inch spike on every digit. He learned that the claws allowed him to pierce stone and brick to scale buildings.

Jude was three quarters of the way up the side of a building, when an arm reached under each of his and lifted him off the side of the skyscraper. He smelled the familiar scent of Michael's sweat. Jude knew that Michael was grinning ear to ear just by hearing his voice. "Get ready for an adrenaline rush."

He arced up and back. When they were 50 feet from the building, Michael let go of Jude.

Jude screamed, "Are you crazy?" He was unable to hear Michael's laughter over the rushing air. Rotating, he turned to face the ground. Jude grasped for straws to solve how he was going to keep from becoming an abstract painting on the pavement. He felt pins and needles up his spine and into his brain. It seemed another entity was present within his body. "Could that be the armor?" He tried to speak with it through thought. *Who are you*? Silence.

Just had 60 feet remaining when he thought, *I could really use a good set of wings right now.*

The tingling in his body shifted from random to waves flowing from his head to his limbs. He then heard the rattling of metal and, what sounded like, the opening of an umbrella. Glancing back, he saw a large wing with countless metal feathers. Before he could process how to use them, the wings shifted and he no longer plummeted towards the ground but flew parallel to it.

A familiar form flew into view and Michael's laugh rang in his ears. Michael flew between two buildings and began bounding from one to the other, working his way up to the roof.

Jude thought, *Let's see what you can do*. In response, the armor angled him towards the buildings that Michael had started scaling. As he planted his feet and sprang off the masonry, the wings began working with the actions of his body for the optimum response.

He heard Michael from the rooftop above. "Push harder, Jude! You need to push yourself to get more speed! That beast is bulky, but that's it's deception! You know, as well as I do, that it is faster than what we gave it credit for during our last skirmish!"

Jude dug deep and started pushing off the buildings with all of his strength. He then heard Michael's voice as it grew ever closer. "That's more like it! Much better! Remember, healing here is almost instantaneous! You're fatigued muscles will heal and grow stronger!"

Jude had already noticed the difference in his body since they had arrived at the grounds. His body felt as if he had been training for months. As he crested the rooftop, his wings set him down in front of Michael. "It's about time you got up here."

"Yeah, yeah. I know. I wasn't pushing myself to my limits."

Michael stepped to his side and placed his hand on Jude's shoulder. "You're doing well. Have you noticed or felt any change in your abilities?"

He nodded and gave a sideways glance at Michael as they began walking towards the opposite side of the building. "As a matter of fact, I didn't notice anything until just a few moments ago, when you urged me to push myself harder."

Michael gave a sullen nod. "You're going to need it." As their eyesight crested to view the street below, they saw Adam slithering and thrashing against wave upon wave of opponents. "We all will. This foe may not turn, as Adam did. Every one of us must be willing to fight to the death."

While both watched Adam, Jude asked, "Do you think he's ready?"

"Yes. He has yet to reach his full potential for his body and armor. He'll unlock it, when the time is right."

"Will it be during this battle?"

Michael's brow furrowed. "That all depends on him, when his body and armor deem the change necessary."

"Will it be something we'll need to watch him extra close when it occurs?"

Michael pursed his lips. "Yes, but only the need to stay out of his way."

Jude looked at Michael. "Is it going to be that drastic?"

Michael shrugged his shoulders. "Hard to say. All I've been told is that it will be extreme."

Jude looked back at Adam. "What do you have in store for us?"

"What indeed." Michael's eyebrow rose. "It's time." He jumped from the building and Jude followed. "Hopefully, the training was enough."

# Chapter 41

C hristophe stepped out onto the lamplit sidewalk from the lobby. He inhaled the chilly night air and grinned as he stepped forward to walk to his destination.

He figured that he would take his time and enjoy the walk through the streets to allow the anticipation to build for the coming carnage. The snow began to fall as he passed all types of people. Christophe saw parents walking hand in hand with children, men in business suits, college aged people in hoodies, and a few homeless people. Every person he passed, he could hear their heartbeat and taste the scent of their flesh.

As he cleared the buildings and the park came into view, his eyes morphed. Christophe heard music and noticed flashing lights and a crowd gathered in front of a stage. With a malicious grin he began walking towards the concert. The closer he got to the venue, the better he could hear the sound of distorted guitars and wicked percussion. The thought that the metal band on stage didn't sound half bad brushed through his mind quickly. He almost felt regret that this would be their last show.

The voice rang out in his mind as he drew near the gates. *"Don't change, until the perfect moment."*

His eyes reverted to human form as he walked up to someone standing at the gate. He took out his wallet. "How much for a ticket?"

The man looked at him and, seeing his suit and tie, raised an eyebrow. "25 bucks."

Christophe removed a 20-dollar bill and a five-dollar bill from his wallet and handed them to the man. The man handed him his ticket and gestured him through with an upturned palm.

He walked through the gate and began making his way towards the stage. As the crowd thickened, he had to more forcefully push his way through. He began nudging and elbowing his way through people. Christophe was about 20 feet from the stage, when a man he tried to elbow past connected with a right cross. The man's eyes went wide as Christophe looked as if he had just adjusted his head to look at something off to the side. He crept his head back in the man's direction and looked into the man's eyes with golden, reptilian eyes. Christophe grinned as the man started backing away trying to flee. With the density of the crowd, the man did not make it far. Christophe's fist connected under the man's chin and lifted him off the ground and hurled him over six of the people in the crowd. Thinking the man was attempting to crowd surf, his unconscious body never touched the ground.

Christophe chuckled, turned, and continued making his

way to the stage. Once he reached the front, he found that security had set up a barrier five feet back from the stage. He had emerged right in front of one of the people working security. Placing his hand on the back of the guard's head, he extended a single claw through the neck at the base of the skull severing the man's spinal cord. As the man fell, he leapt over the railing and onto the stage in a single bound.

Once on the stage, he started acting like he was hyping up the crowd as if he was part of the show. He started pumping his fist in the air. As he was standing five feet from the lead singer, he transformed into his monstrous form. The crowd cheered, until he spun his body 180 degrees and connected with the lead singer launching him halfway towards the back of the crowd.

The music stopped abruptly and the crowd grew quiet in their confusion. He turned towards the back of the stage. As he drew in his breath, the drummer saw one side of the beast's mouth raise in a sneer.

A moment passed and the drummer was frozen in terror. The jaws spread, the frills illuminated, and a stream of molten orange covered the drummer and his kit. The cymbals melted and dripped inward from their edges. The drum skins instantly melted and ignited their interiors. The drummer melted behind a curtain of canned flames.

The bassist and guitarists ran backstage and out of sight. Christophe turned and faced the crowd. He was greeted with countless eyes, wide with terror. A drop of orange dripped from his mouth and sizzled through the stage as the smoke and flames climbed the backdrop. The crowd scattered as his roar bellowed throughout the venue. He leapt from the stage and stalked after the crowd tearing people apart as he made his way back towards the buildings and streets of the city.

# CHAPTER 42

Michael, Adam, and Jude reappeared in the mortal world. As Jude and Adam looked around, they saw an expansive room with full, floor to ceiling, windows overlooking the city. Jude walked over to the windows to see what was visible. Millennium Park and The Navy Pier could be seen in the distance.

Adam and Michael stepped up to his side. Jude said, "It all seems like it's normal flow. Is it getting ready to change?"

Michael gave a snipped, "Yep."

"You say that so casually. Is it going to happen soon?"

Michael shrugged his shoulders. "Hard to say. It could happen any second or within a few hours."

Jude nodded and Adam's brow furrowed. "Knowing Lucius, you're probably right. He does like to keep people guessing."

Michael chuckled. "He's not the only one."

Jude and Adam chuckled. Jude said, "So, you do mess with us on purpose." He looked at Michael's reaction.

Michael lifted one shoulder. "Only about half of the time. The other half is just my personality coming out."

Jude looked back at the streets below. "Who would have guessed?"

From a few blocks over, like the ripples in a pond, a wave of people began running in all directions.

Michael sighed. "Well boys, there's our cue."

Adam responded. "It would seem like it." All three turned to leave the floor, only to find a familiar, clean-cut form stood facing them. Adam greeted him. "Hello, Lucius." He glanced at Jude and Michael. "You two, go ahead. I'll stay here and keep him company."

Michael asked, "Are you sure?"

"Yep. It'll give us a chance to catch up. Besides, I've been waiting for a rematch."

Michael glanced at Lucius as his face lowered and stretched into a wicked sneer. He looked back at Adam. "Just be careful."

Adam turned and glared at Lucius. "Will do."

Michael and Jude moved past Lucius towards the stairs. Adam heard their voices echoing from the darkness. Jude asked in a higher tone than his normal, "Is he going to be okay?"

"Who? Lucius or Adam?"

"Wait! Are you siding with Lucius?"

"Of course not. Adam, will be fine."

The door closed muffling their voices.

Lucius said, "It's been a while, since we've talked one on

one." He clasped his hands behind his back and began walking towards the windows. "Are you sure you're not wanting to join me again?" He stepped up to the window and looked down upon the frantic crowds.

Adam turned and looked out of the window making sure to keep focused on Lucius' reflection. He sighed. "Nope. I'm quite content and happy with how my life is at the moment."

Lucius shrugged and furrowed his brow as he pulled his cigarettes from his pocket. He removed one and placed it between his lips. "Fair enough." With smooth motions, Lucius returned the pack to his pocket and lit the cigarette in his mouth. He inhaled and removed it from his mouth. "You may be happy now, but before the night is over, that will change."

"What's that supposed to mean?"

"My boy, it means that no matter how tonight turns out, win or lose, your family will lose."

Adam turned his head to face Lucius' reflection. "Is that a threat to my family?"

Lucius gave a soft laugh. "No, my dear, boy. It's a guarantee." He placed his hand on Adam's shoulder sending shivers down Adam's spine. "Whether you win or lose tonight your family will feel the effects."

"Who's your pawn this time?"

He took another hit from his cigarette. "I'm not at liberty to say."

Adam nodded. He placed his hand on Lucius' shoulder. "It figures that you'd not give me a straightforward answer." Adam moved his hand from Lucius' shoulder to his neck with a blur. He pulled back and, with a loud hiss, slammed Lucius' head into the glass window causing a web to radiate from the impact point.

Lucius laughed. "That's more like it. There's the temper

that I remember so fondly." He raised his arm up and back. It connected with Adam's arm, breaking his hold on Lucius' neck and forcing it away. He swung his other hand across and up into Adam's gut. Adam grunted and took a step back. "Tell you what, let's play a game. Why don't we stay in human form, and see how much abuse your body can take?" He grinned as he stood up facing Adam.

Adam smirked. "Granted, I'm for it, but how would that be fair?"

Lucius raised an eyebrow. "How would that not be fair?"

"I'm mortal. You're not."

Lucius grinned and nodded. "Ah, yes. That minor dilemma. Well, I guess it'll make it that much more of a challenge for you then. Besides, given who I am, I've never played fair."

Adam nodded. "Yeah. Well, there is that." He started swinging his arm in small circles at his side to loosen it up a bit. "In that case, let's get started."

Lucius grinned and charged at Adam. He tucked and tried to set himself up for a low body shot. Adam correctly read his attempt and stepped to the side and connected with an upper cut to Lucius' chin. The force of the hit and the surge of power left Adam baffled. His blow connected with enough force to throw Lucius into the window, knocking a few glass shards loose and cracking it even more. He turned his head grinding glass into his scalp. His eyes narrowed and he growled with laughter as he grinned at Adam. He stood up and brushed crystalline dust from his arms. "You've improved."

Adam settled into a defensive stance. "Well, that does tend to happen when one trains."

Lucius's grin stretched to inhuman proportions.

"Training can, almost always, be trumped by experience." He held up his hands with all his fingers pointed upwards and curled them back and forth, inviting Adam to advance.

Adam took a slow breath, exhaled, and accepted Lucius' invitation. He lunged forward with controlled steps, thinking he was keeping himself closed off from attacks. Lucius crouched and charged with a blur. The move was so fast that it was impossible for Adam to react in time. Lucius connected with a punch to Adam's gut. As Adam recoiled an inch or two, Lucius opened his hand and raised it under Adam's arm. As his palm connected with Adam's armpit, he clamped his claws into Adam's flesh. He continued the momentum and, one handedly, lifted Adam off his feet, flung him over his head, and body slammed him onto the floor.

Adam felt all the air expend from his lungs. He tried to pause before breathing in, but, before he could, Lucius grabbed his wrist. "You see what experience and immortal powers can give you?"

Lucius started spinning him in circles on the floor. "Let me show you more." Lucius maneuvered Adam against the momentum, lifted him off the ground, flung him back, and launched him forward. Adam felt Lucius' grip release from his wrist, before flying into the webbed window. It gave enough to where one elbow was through the glass, holding him in place.

A millisecond later, Lucius instantly changed form, charged, and speared Adam through the window. As Adam began his plummet and Lucius took flight, he heard his voice fade away as they grew distant. "Enjoy your fall from grace and life, moron."

# CHAPTER 43

As the door closed behind Jude, Michael paused. Jude stopped, "What?"

He started heading upstairs instead of down. "Just had to think whether we were closer to the roof or the lobby."

"I had figured that's what you were doing." They kept climbing. As they started the last few flights of stairs, Jude asked, "Do you truly not know who we're up against, or are you keeping it from us?"

Michael responded as they approached the door to the roof. "You're getting smarter." He opened the door and pushed it wide to give Jude time to run through without it hitting him. "Of course, I know who we're up against."

"Then why not tell us?"

"Because, even the slightest risk of it affecting people's

judgement, may cost milliseconds that could risk lives. Everyone will know the beast's identity when the time is right."

They stepped up to the building edge.

"That sounds like a valid reason to remain silent."

Michael looked over the edge. "Whole different experience when you're able to fly, isn't it?"

"Hadn't really thought about it until now, but, yeah. It actually is... Michael."

"Yeah."

"...what are we waiting on?"

Michael held up his hand. "This." He pointed down a second before Adam's elbow shot through the window, followed a split second later by Lucius and the rest of Adam's body. Jude stepped up to jump and Michael put his palm on Jude's chest. "Wait."

"He's falling to his death!"

"Give him a few seconds. If nothing happens... then we go."

Jude's breathing came shallow and rapid as he watched his friend plummeting towards the street below. Jude was just about ready to jump when he noticed a difference in Adam's appearance. "Now, we can go." They both stepped off the side and dove headfirst. They kept a keen eye on Adam as they dropped. As he changed, he maintained his typical light blue coloration, but his scales and body were much thicker. Two massive wings sprouted from his back. A pair of bulky legs and human like arms grew from his body. His head became spiked and squarer in shape than his snake form. He caught the wind with his wings and leveled off.

Michael and Jude extended their wings. Jude looked over to Michael. "A dragon? Seriously? You all couldn't come up with something different?"

Michael smirked and changed course to head towards the beast's location. "Are you jealous?"

Jude laughed. "Truthfully?" He smiled. "Yeah."

Michael flew over Adam's head and yelled out, "It's about time you figured out your new form. Way to be a late bloomer." He flew farther out in front of Adam. Adam breathed a short burst of white mist that engulfed Michael's feet. He pulled them in and started rubbing them to warm them back up. "Hey! That's not funny!"

Jude flew a few feet above Adam. Adam rolled and stretched his arm and high fived Jude mid barrel roll. He leveled off and snorted mist from his nostrils as he chuckled.

# CHAPTER 44

As the three rounded a corner, the beast came into view two blocks ahead. It stood at its full height and length of 20 feet. The horrific scene grew more gruesome the closer they got. The monster stood in the middle of the street clutching a wriggling and screaming person in each reptilian hand with a trail of dead bodies strewn behind it.

Christophe looked up at the approaching forms, extended his frills, and shook them. He slammed the heads of the people in his hands into two parked cars on either side of him. The heads separated from the bodies, and he tossed them over the cars with ribbons of crimson streaming in their wake. He crouched down, ready for the oncoming threat.

As they drew closer, a dark cloud started heading straight for them from a higher altitude than what they were flying.

Michael watched as the mass passed over his head. He realized as he flew under it, that it was a legion of winged demons. Michael continued on thinking it had passed over the three of them. The mass beyond over Michael and Adam, but swarmed Jude.

As Jude began his struggle with the swarm, Michael and Adam continued forward. Adam was focusing on the beast ahead of them, when a familiar form dropped from above. Its feet connected with Michael's back and drove him down towards the pavement below. Knowing that Michael could handle his own in a fight with Lucius, Adam continued over their free-falling bodies. As he neared the monster, he slowed his breathing and focused on the beast's movements to try and get a read on it. The beast began jumping up and down to limber up for the fight to come.

Jude's eyes focused on a black swarm ahead of them. His ears registered the hum of countless wings as the mass drew closer. He angled his wings up to catch the wind and loop backwards as the swarm surrounded him and started attacking. Jude flexed his fingers, and his claws illuminated the darkness.

His arms began swinging in attempts to connect with anything. With every swipe of his claws, multiple bodies disintegrated in explosions of embers and ash. He began diving and rising through the deafening cloud leaving gray and orange trails in his wake from his outstretched arms.

The mass followed his every movement. He angled towards a building and sank his claws through two demons and into the building. Jude looked around to see the scope of the challenge he was facing. The group were so great in number that a third of them were on the side of the building and the other building was blocked from view from the other two thirds.

* * *

As Michael watched the ground approaching, he reacted with a subtle, but quick, movement. Extending one wing, he created enough drag to roll himself out from under Lucius' force. As Lucius extended his leathery wings to stop his decent, he unsheathed a black, gnarled looking sword from his back.

Michael distanced himself from Lucius and pulled his sword and shield as they hovered in mid-air facing each other. Lucius snarled. "You still have some fight in you."

Michael smirked. "That I do, but I also know that you do as well." He reversed the positioning of his sword, so the blade pointed behind him. "Let's see what you've got."

They both flew towards each other and closed the gap. Lucius attempted to strike an upward blow and Michael took advantage of the opening. He rolled left, missing the blade. He tucked his wings to glide under Lucius' right wing. As he moved past Lucius, he extended his arm and sliced down Lucius' torso.

Lucius let out a bellowing roar and tried to slash sideways at Michael. His swing found only air. Michael turned to face Lucius from a safe distance. He could see a stream of smoking black liquid running from the Devil's side.

Black ooze started seeping from Lucius' free hand and began hardening upon itself. When it had finished, he was left with a long shield emblazoned with a giant goat's head.

Michael reversed his grip on the sword again. He shook his head. "With how little you use that, I'm shocked you haven't swapped it for another."

Lucius looked at his shield and then back at Michael. He shrugged. "It's reliable."

Michael laughed. "Are you sure that it's not rusted through?"

"Are you scared that you're going to get tetanus? Why don't you come test it and see?"

Michael grinned and charged forward.

* * *

After the beast stopped jumping up and down, it crouched almost into a wrestling stance. Adam knew that it was ready for him. The monster flared its frills. Adam saw them and its mouth glow bright orange. It spit a stream of molten liquid and coated a line from one building wall to the opposing building wall. Everything the material touched ignited or smoldered.

As Adam neared the wall of smoke and flame, he knew that it was only a few minutes before the gas tanks would ignite and possibly lead to domino effect explosions with the other parked cars.

Flying towards the beast and flames, he had a moment to react. He breathed deep and flew straight at the wall of smoke. A few seconds before hitting the plume of smoke, he engulfed the flames and debris in a cloud of ice crystals and mist. The air between buildings turned from black to a foggy yellow.

Adam changed course and went vertical at the edge of the fog. Christophe waited on the other side for Adam to pierce through the cloud. A second or two after he expected Adam to attack, he began looking around for his opponent. He was just about to hide in the shadows to catch is son-in-law by surprise when an immense weight collapsed on top of him, pinning him to the ground.

He was able to turn his head enough to see a massive, turquoise scaled dragon standing over him. The creature had him held down with one of its arms.

Christophe struggled to gain the upper hand and get free of Adam's grasp. When his efforts proved fruitless, he began thinking of other options for escape. He realized after a second, that his tail was still free.

Adam leaned toward Christophe and, in a growling non-human tone, asked, "Who are you?"

Christophe looked up and grinned. He then lashed his tail under Adam's arm and up the side of his neck, coating it in acid.

As it began eating through his scales, Adam looked down and said, "Your tail won't do you any good."

In response Christophe held his tail up in front of Adam's face. He flicked his tail flinging a few droplets of acid onto a nearby car. Adam watched the droplets fly off and start sizzling away at one of the nearby vehicles. Corrosive vapors burned Adam's nostrils just as the acid reached his skin. He roared in pain, then looked down at Christophe. His face stretched into a grin as he took in the ferocity seething within Adam's eyes. Adam lifted him into the air and threw him into a parked van, knocking it over and through a department store window.

Adam lifted his hand towards his neck and thought better of it at the last second. He panicked a moment before thinking of looking for a water source. After a second or two of looking over the buildings, his eyes set upon a fire hydrant a block away. He made it two steps in its direction, when the full mass of Christophe's body leapt from the shattered window and onto Adam's back.

Christophe stood between Adam's shoulder blades and began clawing at Adam's back. The longer he tried, the more frustrated he became. The armor blocked any attacks that he attempted. Christophe then began lashing with his tail. The acid had no effect on the armor, but, just as he was about it give up on his efforts, he saw a drop of acid roll between the armor plates.

Adam felt the beast start lashing all over with his tail. It tried to focus on his damaged neck and his wings and arms. He took flight in hopes of knocking the beast off his back and to its death. Adam made it six stories into the air when the skin beneath his armor started screaming, as the acid ate through the membrane of his wings. He saw windows passing with increased speed as he plummeted to the pavement below. Christophe jumped from his back at the last second.

Adam's back now faced the fog. Christophe spun to face him, after he slowed to a stop. He grinned as Adam tried to rise and failed. Christophe could now see red coating the side of Adam's neck and see purple lines coming from under his armor.

He laughed. In a voice that sounded half reptilian hiss and half raven's croak, he said, "You're pathetic. I am going to enjoy killing you. Maybe, I'll go after that pretty wife of yours and your brats next." He spread his frills and inhaled. As his throat and frills began to glow, a large furry form jumped between him and Adam.

Christophe paused and began exhaling smoke from his nostrils as the red panda stared him in the eyes. It slowly shook its head as Christophe finished exhaling. He gave a quick sniff of the air. His mouth stretched into a sneering grin. "Well, isn't this an unexpected surprise. Today's my lucky day. I've always loved the practice of leaving no loose ends."

He breathed in once again until his eyes, mouth, and frills radiated orange light. He let loose a torrent of molten material.

# CHAPTER 45

Jude tried to calculate attack after attack. He had attempted flying building to building while slashing and stabbing with his claws, turning the demons to ash. Flying to the rooftops and diving towards the street below, he tried extending his arms and illuminated claws outward as he dove. This succeeded in taking out quite a few of his winged foes, but more always seemed to emerge from the shadows.

His brain turned over and over for a logical solution to gaining the upper hand over the swarm. He was grateful that the armor was, for the most part, protecting him from attacks.

Jude spoke to himself among the din of demonic screeches. "What am I missing?" A demon hovered in front of his face grinning. It swung an open palm towards his face. He blocked the blow and swiped through its body. "This can't be the extent of this armor's powers." He clawed through another demon's face as he realized he should be mindful of his verbalizations around their enemies.

As he focused on the war outside and his internal confusion, a secondary mass of demons shifted away from the cloud surrounding Jude. They distanced themselves five stories higher and half a block away. It arced back and javelined itself at Jude. The wall around Jude parted at the last second before the swarm collided. Jude had enough time to face the onslaught. He tried clawing through a few of them, but was being shot backwards by a multitude of winged bodies with momentum behind them. A millisecond before impact against one of the buildings, the armor acted of its own accord and extended its wings. It emitted a light as a concussion wave burst out of the armor against the building, lessening the force of Jude's impact. A few of the demons in Jude's immediate vicinity disintegrated from the light. The ones farther out, turned and flew a few feet away from Jude.

Seeing that he was still surrounded, he dropped and allowed gravity to increase his gap and distance himself from the swarm. At what he first thought was intuition, something told him to trust the armor.

He shifted from a fall into a dive. The solution had been with him the entire time. "How could I have forgotten already?" It had dawned on him that he only needed to trust and have faith in his armor; it knew its own capabilities.

As he reached the street below, he ran a few steps to see if the swarm was following. Jude knew before he turned back that it was closing in on him. He could hear the demonic cries and the low whine of approaching wings. As he caught sight of the mass, he turned and took shelter under the armor's wings.

A barrage of claws and teeth began to assault the wings and although the armor protected his exposed areas, and occasional hand would make it through the armor's defenses. His internal struggle continued as his human side wanted to try and flee, but he knew he had to trust the armor. On the verge of impatience at waiting for the armor to react, it finally took action. Outside of Jude's cover, it looked like a giant black, skittering dome that rose three stories tall. A shock wave of blinding light detonated from the armor. A split second later, the dome was obliterated into a cloud of smoke and flittering embers.

Jude stood and looked around. "Well, now that that's taken care of..." He looked back and saw more figures crawling out of the shadows. "Then again." The icy cloud from Adam's breath caught his eye. The armor responded that it trusted his judgement and he took flight for the fog.

\* \* \*

Michael hovered with his sword and shield hanging at his sides. He grinned at Lucius. "Do you prefer to keep up the acrobatics, or do you prefer to continue this at ground level?" Lucius lifted his feet out behind him and began flying head-first towards Michael. He raised his sword and shield. "Aerial it is."

As Lucius neared, Michael awaited his opportunity. The Devil gained more speed as he neared. Lucius held his sword close to his body with its tip extending beyond his head. He held it with both hands, so that his shield protected his chest and stomach. Before Lucius' sword could connect with the shield, Michael leveled out and flew over Lucius carving down Lucius' spine with his sword.

Lucius slowed and screamed in pain as Michael continued in a backward arc bringing his feet down on Lucius' back directly on the fresh wound. Lucius tucked his wings in and raised his legs toward Michael. He wrapped his legs around Michael and pulled into an inverted sit-up. Lucius pulled his torso 270 degrees and slammed his shield into Michael's face and body with its force. He released Michael.

The impact jolted Michael and caused him to fall 20 feet before reorienting himself and flying a few feet away. He looked to the void where Lucius had been. Michael searched his surroundings for his former brother.

Lucius hovered above him moving out of view with every movement of Michael's searching. He threw his sword and shield onto his back. He leaned back into a reverse dive, dropped until he was near Michael, and spread his wings to right himself before colliding with Michael. He grabbed Michael's wings and collapsed them. He then flipped into another reverse dive. Michael tried to strike Lucius with blows from his sword and shield without success.

Michael and Lucius watched as the pavement drew closer. "Well, Michael, you seem obsessed with fighting at ground level. Allow me to grant you your request." Just before their heads slammed into the asphalt, Lucius pulled up so that Michael took the full force of the fall with Lucius' weight and momentum added.

Lucius glided 30 feet away and gently landed in the middle of the street. Michael, facing away from the fog, struggled to his feet. Blood ran from his nose and mouth. He brought his sword hand up and wiped the back of his thumb across his upper lip and smiled at the sight of his own blood.

Lucius grinned. "You may as well give up. You're outnumbered and the other two are mortal. I can guarantee that they will die if you choose to keep fighting."

As Michael looked at Lucius, he watched behind the Devil at the same time. After seeing Jude dive to the street, he nodded and sheathed his sword. "Well, Lucius, you know how I am. I've always loved the challenge of daunting odds. Besides," The dome of demons vaporized. Lucius' eyes flitted to the side at the flash of light. Jude took flight in their direction. "...these mortals may surprise you."

Lucius glanced up as Jude flew over his head and towards the fog. Michael shot into the air on Jude's heels. Lucius snarled and followed after them ahead of his demons.

\* \* \*

Adam wondered why Shannon would sacrifice herself to allow him to survive. He thought back to Jess' stories that she always thought of her like a mom or an aunt. He saw her shake her head at the beast just before it inhaled.

As the beast's mouth, eyes, and frills glowed orange, he felt regret at not being able to stop this menace and that Shannon was going to give her life senselessly. With how deep the beast was inhaling, he knew it would take them both out within the next few moments.

The beast rattled its frills and started spitting its incinerating material. Just as it did, the fog behind Adam exploded with white light. He saw a silhouette fly over his head and slam into the pavement between the beast and Shannon. When the figure came to a stop, he saw Michael crouched with his shield blocking the full force of the monster's attack.

A charred figure with smoldering wings tumbled through the fog, rolled, and struggled on the ground gasping for air.

Michael turned to Shannon and nodded. As the creature was expelling the last of its molten stream, Shannon ran out and around it. She darted up his back and perched atop his head.

Michael's shield glowed orange as he stood. He and Adam watched as Shannon began clawing at Christophe's eyes, damaging them beyond use. Christophe screeched in pain and grabbed Shannon and catapulted her into a nearby car.

Christophe raised his hand to his eyes and roared. His nostrils flared as he sniffed the air. He could still smell the blood from Adam's wounds and knew they were still concentrated in the same place. Christophe also noticed a different scent moving away. He thought, *Ah, yes, the ally. Well, if I can't take them both out, I'll still be able to take out that worthless son-in-law of mine.*

He shook his frills and stuttered a few breaths in and out to reignite the fire in his throat. Michael had taken flight and hovered about 50 feet in the air. Christophe sneered as he let loose with another torrent of molten rock.

Adam lifted his head and countered with a stream of misting ice. As they connected the molten material hardened and was overtaken by Adam's defense. The arctic blast engulfed Christophe, hardening the material in his body and freezing the outside of his body at the same time.

Michael dove with his sword drawn. His blade connected with the back of Christophe's neck and severed through it as Michael swung down under him and launched himself out and landed in front of Lucius.

As the massive body thudded to the ground, Michael said, "You see, brother, I always love daunting odds. They usually have the most surprising outcomes." He tapped the tip of his sword on the ground. "See you soon." Michael raised the sword and plunged it through Lucius' temple. He ignited into embers and was gone.

Jude stepped from the fog and ran to check on Adam. "Are you okay?"

"I need water."

"You just need a drink. Are you kidding me?"

Adam shook his head. "Acid. It secreted acid from its tail. Find water to neutralize it."

Jude nodded. "Got it."

Michael called after him, "Jude." Jude looked towards him. He threw his shield to him. "Use this." Jude caught the shield and ran for the nearest hydrant. Michael walked over to Adam. "You doing okay?"

"Yeah, just in a lot of pain." He looked to see Shannon with green and white coloration, breathing on deep scratches she acquired when thrown by Christophe. "I'm more worried about Shannon. Is she going to be okay?"

"I'm sure she will be." They watched as her wounds started to mend and scar over. She rose and walked towards Christophe's head. When she reached it, she sat down and pressed the top of her head against his. Her color changed from green to black. "I'll go check on her."

As Jude arrived and poured water over Adam's wounds, Michael sat down next to Shannon and placed his hand on her shoulder. A few minutes later, Shannon lifted her head and looked over in Adam's direction. Her and Michael began walking towards them. Shannon's color morphed to dark green.

She immediately walked to Adam's wounds and started working on healing them. "I'm sorry." Shannon gave a slow nod. "You must have been close to him." Another slow nod.

Her eyes clinched shut and tears dropped to the ground as she continued mending his wounds.

Jude handed Michael his shield. "You alright?" Michael asked.

Jude sighed. "Yeah, Lucius threw a ton at us this time. Didn't he?"

Michael nodded and turned to look at Christophe's scaled body. "That he did."

Adam looked at Michael. "So, who was it?"

Shannon stopped and turned towards Michael. He looked at her as she shook her head. "That will be revealed to you when the time is right." Shannon nodded, turned, and continued to heal Adam's wounds.

When Adam's wounds were healed a few minutes later, Shannon walked up to Michael and placed her paw on his shoulder. Michael turned and looked at her. "He all healed up?" She nodded. "Thank you. Why don't you go on home to get some rest? I'll be by later to talk." He placed his hand on the fur between her eyes and a tear rolled down his cheek. "I'm truly sorry." She nodded and walked through the mist and out of sight.

Michael turned to Adam. "How did you manage to pull off that last maneuver without breathing in?"

"Who said I didn't? As soon as you blocked that first attack, I started to inhale through my nostrils so I would be able to pull it off with not having the strength to move much."

Michael looked at Jude. "Well, it seems like he has a few surprises up his sleeve as well." He laughed. "Why don't you head on back to the hotel and get some rest. Jude and I can finish things up here."

"Are you sure?"

"I'm certain." He flicked his hands outward. "Go on.

We'll be along shortly."

Adam nodded and walked towards the hotel, returning to human form while in the mist.

# CHAPTER 46

A dam walked through the door of the hotel room to see a familiar figure standing by the window looking out over the city. "Jess?"

She didn't turn. "Yeah."

He stood at the edge of the room. "I thought you were in New York."

Her voice came back monotone and distant. "I was, but I caught a turnaround flight."

Adam nodded and looked around. "Where are the boys?"

"They are safe. I left them in Simon's care."

"Simon?" He asked with a raised brow. The reference at dinner before their training flashed back into his head. Adam tried his best to act like he was ignorant that Simon met her at the airport.

"Someone that I was told could be trusted."

"Hopefully by a reliable source."

"I don't need your attitude right now, Adam." She wiped at her cheek. "Besides, I wouldn't leave them in a strangers care otherwise."

Adam looked at his feet. "Fair enough. I trust your judgement." He looked back up at her. "Why did you come back?"

"I had some unfinished business to attend to."

"Christophe?"

She turned with tears streaming down her face. "Yeah."

"Were you able to find him?"

She covered her mouth to hold back her sobs and nodded. "He was beyond saving."

"I'm sure he isn't. People change every day. Just give him time."

"It's too late for that now." She winced as she lifted her shirt to reveal, freshly healed, claw marks across her side. "Shannon isn't the Red Panda. I am. He proved tonight that he was beyond saving." Her brow furrowed as she collapsed to her knees.

He walked over to her, sat, and held her as the pieces began fitting together in his mind. He cried with her for the pain she was going through and the gravity of the combination of all the events of recent days. He was angry and hurt that she had carried a burden so heavy over the past few weeks. Adam could only empathize with the amount of betrayal she was feeling. He thought back to the Red Panda's interactions with the beast during, and after, the fight and cried harder.

She pulled out her phone. "I need to call the boys and make sure that they're okay."

"Do you want me to call?"

She wiped her eyes. "No. I need to hear their voices."

"Tell them that I love them."

The phone rang and Simon answered. "Hello."

"Hi, Simon. It's Jessica. Are the boys safe?"

"Hi, Jessica. Yes, they are. They're both asleep at the moment. Do you want me to wake them?"

She shook her head. "No, that's okay. Let them sleep. Thank you for watching them and keeping them safe."

"You're welcome. Let me know if you need anything. Is everything alright there?"

Her voice strained. "As good as it can be. We're all safe, but it'll take a while to mend."

"Glad to hear it. Take all the time you need and keep me posted."

"Will do. Thank you, again."

"It's the least I can do."

They both hung up and she leaned into Adam's good shoulder to continue crying in the safety of his arms.

# CHAPTER 47

J ess, Adam, and the twins sat in the front pew of the church. Statues lined the sanctuary on either side. A large crucifix hung behind the alter looming over Christophe's casket. The priest stood talking to them giving them words of comfort and letting them know how the service would proceed. His mouth quit moving as he saw Michael and Jude walking into the sanctuary. He stepped towards the altar as he addressed them. "My apologies, but the doors for funeral attendees aren't open for another 40 minutes."

Michael responded, "It's alright, Father. We're family."

Recognizing Michael's voice, Jess nodded. "My apologies." He looked back at Jess and Adam and continued. "…in order to heal, you must take time to mourn." Michael and Jude stepped up and stood next to the Priest. "Salt provides healing and that's why tears contain salt. They help heal in times of pain. Not just physically, but emotionally as well." Michael nodded and smirked. "Have you heard that saying before or do you just find it amusing?"

Michael's expression turned stoic. "More times than I care to count, but the saying is true. The smirk was due to remembering giving the same comfort on frequent occasions."

Jess looked up at the priest. "He has a lot of experience with death."

"Are you a priest, counsellor, or a mortician?"

Everyone, but the father and the twins, laughed. Michael smiled. "To be honest, I'm all of the above."

The priest's face grew red thinking he was being lied to. "How is it possible to be a priest and a mortician? You should be giving your full effort to spreading God's message and doing his works." His face turned scarlet as Michael grinned wider.

"Allow me to explain." He stepped towards the Priest and placed his hand on his head with his thumb on the bridge of the priest's nose and his fingertips on the back of his head. Visions of Michael's memories of escorting the departed to the next life filled the priest's mind. He saw wings curl from behind his viewpoint. Michael's voice hummed in his mind. "I am not just *a* mortician; I am *thee* mortician. I have had to comfort countless souls and families throughout history."

While Michael had this connection with the priest, he searched his soul and was glad to find he had led an honest life thus far. Michael removed his thumb and the old priest was back in his sanctuary. His mouth agape, he almost yelled and fell to his knees. The sight of Michael holding a finger to his lips and shaking his head stopped the priest from following through on his urge to show reverence. "My sincerest apologies." He glanced around nervously at the other three.

"It's alright, Father. They know."

His shoulders relaxed. "Well, that explains the laughter." A figure entered the back of the sanctuary. The priest looked at Jess. "Someone else you know?"

Jess turned to see Shannon coming down the aisle. "Yes, Father." She stood up and went to speak with Shannon.

Michael looked at Jude and Jude nodded. "I know what would cheer the two of you up." He walked over to the twins. The boys looked at Jude with red eyes. "Let's go get some ice cream."

They both smiled at Jude. "Can we dad?"

"I won't argue. Just be on your best behavior."

"We will, daddy." Jude picked up a twin in each arm.

Adam mouthed, "Thank you," to Jude who nodded and walked his way up the aisle with the boys.

Michael sat next to Adam. The priest, not knowing what to do, just remained standing in place. "Thank you for wrapping up things with his body and the situation the other night." They both smirked as they watched the color drain from the priest's face with his brow furrowing and starting to fidget.

Michael held up his hand and in a soft voice said, "It's not what you think Arthur." He looked at Adam who raised his brow and tilted his head. "Then again, it is, but it isn-oh, it will just be easier to explain."

"The only reason that I'm not running is the fact I know who you…" He pointed at Michael. "…are."

"Thank you for your respect and composure." He looked at Adam.

Adam looked at Father Arthur. "Do you remember how we told you that Christophe was killed by the monster?" Arthur nodded. "The truth, Father, is that Christophe was the monster."

Father Arthur's mouth dropped open. "What of the other creatures that were pictured with him? Are they a threat? Are they on our side, and if so, are they okay?"

Michael burst out laughing. Adam pulled his collar down. "We're alright, but still healing." The priest's eyes widened at the burn scar spanning the depth of Adam's neck."

"Thank you for fighting for the safety of our city and fighting the Lord's battles. What about the red panda creature that was also pictured? It looked like it had some wounds to it as well."

Adam looked over his shoulder towards Jess. "Her physical wounds are healing, but some wounds run much deeper and take a lifetime to heal."

Father Arthur's brow furrowed. "So, she helped kill her father to save the city and do God's work?" Adam and Michael nodded in unison. "That poor child." He crossed himself as he thought a quick prayer over her.

Michael stood. "Speaking of which, I do need to speak with her."

Adam grabbed his wrist. "Michael." Michael looked at him. "Thank you." Michael patted his hand, Adam released his grip, and Michael walked up the aisle.

Michael approached Shannon and Jess. He placed his hand on the small of Jess' back and extended his other hand. "Hi, I'm Michael."

Shannon clasped his hand. "Nice to meet you, Michael. I'm Shannon."

"Lovely to meet you. Jess has told me so much about you."

"All good things I hope." She smirked as her cheeks reddened.

"Only the best."

Shannon raised her hand to her chest. "My, you are a handsome charmer. Aren't you?"

"I've been told that a time or two. Thank you for the compliment." He turned to Jess. "Do you have a couple of minutes?"

Jess nodded. "Most certainly." She looked back at Shannon. "Thank you for coming. Adam is up front if you'd like to say hi."

"I definitely will." She kissed Jess' cheek and hugged her before heading towards the front of the sanctuary.

Michael escorted Jess over to one of the pews and they both took a seat. "How are you doing?"

"I'm doing alright. My wounds are healing well."

"I'm glad your wounds are healing well, but you know that's not what I was referring to.".

Jess looked at the casket at the front of the sanctuary. "To be honest?"

When she turned her head to look at him, she found an intense pair of eyes looking into hers. They bore into her thoughts and the depths of her soul. "Yes. You need to be."

"I don't know."

"Talk your way through it."

"There are so many thoughts and emotions." Her brow furrowed. "I'm angry, because of his selfishness. I'm also sad for all the possibilities his choices caused him to miss out on. Betrayal, at hearing him say he was going to kill my family and me. Seeing his elation at the prospect of killing me and Adam at the same time." Her tears began streaming as Michael placed his hand on her shoulder. "Why couldn't he be saved like Adam?"

"Because, he didn't want to. He loved the power from it."

He looked at the casket. "In some ways, I wish I could have kept you from knowing."

She dabbed her eyes with a tissue. "Do you think it would have made the burden easier to bear?"

"It's difficult to say. You would have been exposed to a little less, but all these emotions that you're experiencing would have borne down on you in a matter of minutes." He looked at her. "It may have also meant that we would have been forced to keep secrets from you, and I only want honesty among the team."

"You kept Christophe and my identity from them. How is that different?"

Michael nodded and turned to look at Adam and Shannon talking at the front of the church. "We were being cautious. If Adam had known your true identities, it could have caused a moment of hesitation which could have cost us dearly." He looked back at her and she nodded. "All of the emotions that you're reeling with, are valid. Don't dwell on them too much."

"It doesn't stop me from being burdened with them." She stared at the casket; Her expression empty. "Why couldn't he love me?"

"He could not love you, because he could not love himself. He always loved success and power above all else." Michael breathed out slowly. "It's understandable, but don't think of them as a burden." She raised one of her eyebrows. "You're not at fault for Christophe's choices. He was the person to act on them, not you." She looked at her hands resting on her lap. "His sins were his own, just as yours are your own." A tear dropped from her eye.

She whispered, "A child is not guilty for the sins of the parent."

"Exactly. He is the one suffering from his decisions. Your feelings are the result of his choices, which is why you need to process them as part of the mourning process. Get mad, cry, yell, or sit in silence, do what you have to do to work through it. Just don't carry it with you, or it will drag you down. You also have to remember that you aren't walking this path alone."

She dabbed her eyes again. "I know." She leaned into his shoulder and he put his arm around hers.

"Adam is troubled from knowing what you're going through. I know he wishes things could have been reversed or sheltered you from it."

"I know. I could read it in his eyes. Thank you, again, for saving him when you did."

"No thanks needed."

"I was on the verge of leaving him. He has changed so much and has become the husband and father that I had always dreamt he would be." She saw Shannon began crying uncontrollably and Adam started to fidget. "I better get up there. He looks pretty uncomfortable." They both stood and he stepped out into the aisle and gave her room to step out. She kissed him on the cheek.

"Are you feeling a little better after talking?"

"A little, thank you." She started walking towards the front of the church. "There is one thing I've been wondering."

He shifted his head towards her. "Yes?"

"What was his motivation?" She raised her hand to her necklace. Her hand grabbed the pendant and ran it back and forth along its chain. "Why did he make a deal?"

"You mean Christophe?"

"Yeah."

"He owed people a lot of money and figured he could

take them all out, clear his debt, and create a monopoly for himself with the shady activities going on in the city's underground."

"All the over-the-top murders over the last few weeks?"

"They were his doing."

She nodded her head and they continued down the aisle.

# Chapter 48

The group sat in a diner booth when Jess walked up to them. Adam slid over and she sat down. "Sorry that I'm late. The streets are always a bear at this time of day."

Michael smiled. "It's alright as long as we're all here."

Adam said, "I've already placed the order for what you told me."

"Thank you."

"You're welcome."

Michael took a sip of his coffee and looked around the booth. Simon and Jude sat on his left and Adam and Jess to his right. "I'm glad to have you all here. You did well in Chicago," he looked at Simon, "and here." He looked into his coffee cup. "With that being said, we must remain vigilant. Knowing Lucius, he already has his next plan thought out, or has already set it into motion."

Simon took a drink of water. "What should we be looking for?"

"The usual thing that may be tied to Lucius' normal activities."

Jude retorted, "Which is, literally, everything."

Michael chuckled. "Oh, yeah. Look for anything out of the ordinary range of crime within the city, or country. Any unsolved crimes or crimes that have an odd motos operandai behind them, especially if they're unexplainable."

The orders arrived and after the waiter stepped away, Jess said as she poured ketchup for her fries, "I can keep an eye on the news. Anything that seems to raise a red flag, I can start a log of and keep everyone up to date."

"Thank you, Jess. That would be a tremendous help."

Simon said, "I could check with some of my connections and see if they know anything."

Adam responded, "That could help find out a little information. It's not typically his style from what we've seen so far."

Simon's brow furrowed. "What do you mean?"

Adam looked at him. "He already has reign over the criminals. He prefers turning people away from good or preying on those who are weak and vulnerable." He looked at Michael. "On the other hand, he may try to mix it up a little bit to keep us on our toes."

Michael lifted his coffee cup and pointed to Adam. "You have a good point with that." He took a drink of coffee and set his hands on the table, holding the cup between them. "Simon, find out what you can, but be careful." Simon nodded. Michael looked from Jude to Adam. "Jude, are going to do your usual?"

"Watching from the rooftops?"

"Yeah."

"Yep. That and roam the streets to see if anything looks out of sorts."

"Sounds good. Adam? What about you?" Michael asked.

Adam's fingernail scratched the back lip of his cup. "With how nasty it sounds, I think if Jude has above ground, then I can take below ground. I should be able to hear better that way, and still move unseen."

Jess lifted her glass to take a drink. Just before the glass reached her lips, she said, "Looking to relive your days being one of Lucius' pawns?" Everyone smirked and stifled laughter as Simon looked at Adam with wide eyes.

"Good plan. It would give us a better advantage whenever Lucius decides to start his next scheme."

Adam looked at Michael. "Are we good with the plan?"

Michael pursed his lips and gave a quick, few nods. "It sounds like it."

"Good." He looked at Simon. "Do I have something in my teeth or on my collar?"

"Not that I can see from here. Why do you ask?"

"Oh, you know, no reason. You've just been staring at me for the last five minutes or so."

A smile curled up one side of his mouth. "I wasn't staring at you."

Adam's brow furrowed and he turned to look over his shoulder. A boy with sand colored hair stood on his knees facing their booth. He tried to hide behind Adam's shoulder staring wide eyed at Simon.

Adam turned in his seat to look at the little boy. His mom said, "I am so sorry. James, sit down and eat your lunch."

"He's fine ma'am. We have two boys of our own." The

mother gave a soft nod.

"How old are they?"

"They're six."

Another nod. "He's five."

Adam looked at James. "That's great. You're five?"

James nodded slowly while keeping his eyes glued on Simon. He leaned over and whispered in Adam's ear. "What is wrong with him?"

"James!" She looked at Simon. "I am so sorry."

Adam grinned and pointed at Simon. "Him?"

"Yeah."

"He is cursed from not obeying his mom or dad."

James' eyes flew open. "James, sit down and eat your food." The boy paused and, taking one last look at Simon, spun and started eating his food. The mom raised her eyebrows and pursed her lips. "Well, I guess that's one way to get him to listen." The table laughed. "Again, I am so sorry."

Simon smiled. "No apology needed."

# EPILOGUE

J essica put on her coat. She grabbed her purse, keys, and
a couple envelopes from the island. She walked out of
the apartment and locked the door behind her. She had
wanted to watch more of the news to see if any activity would
stand out, but there were errands that needed ran before she
picked the boys up from daycare.

She stopped by the building's mail boxes to mail the envelopes. Jess then made her way to the parking garage.

As she approached her car, she noticed a young girl in
ragged clothing sitting against a pillar. The girl sat so still that
Jess wondered if she was asleep or dead. "Excuse me." She
bent down a little to try and see the girl's face. At the sound
of her voice the girl opened her eyes and shifted a blank gaze
at Jessica. "Are you okay?"

She gave a slow shake of her head and answered in a

meek voice. "Not really, no."

"Can I help you in any way?" She walked closer to the girl and knelt down. "If there is any way that I can help you, I'm more than willing too." She touched her hand to the girl's shoulder. The girl turned and looked at Jessica's hand on her shoulder and then back to Jess. She pulled her hand back. "I'm sorry."

The girl tilted her head and her eyes brightened. "Actually," She rose to her feet and Jess stood with her. "...there is something that you could help me with." A chill ran down Jess' spine as she watched the girl fade from sight.

The first blow was blinding as the girl attacked, unseen. Jess saw no shadow or warping of the space around her. The second blow knocked her out and left her vulnerable for further assault.

\* \* \*

Michael landed outside of the parking garage and ran inside. He ran to check if Jess' car was still in its parking spot. Seeing that it was in the parking spot, he started to turn to go check their apartment. A glimpse of a human hand caught his eye between the wall and the front bumper.

He ran around the car to find Jessica laying in a pool of blood. Michael knelt down and placed his hand on her head. He felt the vibration from a slow, weak breath. He knelt scooped her and her belongings up in his arms.

As he flew out of the parking garage, he looked at her. His voice was panicked and worried. "Hang on, Jess. I'll get help soon. I'm going to take you to the hospital." Michael sped past buildings heading towards the hospital.

*Aaron D. Brinker* is an author of stories in a variety of genres. He enjoys adding depth and meaning into his stories, while also dabbling in the macabre and twisted.

www.aaronbrinker.com

https://twitter.com/aarondbrinker
https://www.facebook.com/aarondbrinker